MW01128039

A Surplus of Light

A Novel by Chase Connor

Chase Connor Books

The Lion Fish Press

www.chaseconnor.com

www.thelionfishpress.com

CHASE CONNOR BOOKS are published by:

The Lion Fish Press
539 W. Commerce St #227
Dallas, TX 75208

AUTHORS' NOTE:
This is a work of fiction. Names, characters, places, and incidents either are the product of the authors' imagination or are used fictitiously, and any resemblance to actual persons, living or dead, business establishments, events, or locales is entirely coincidental. None of this is real. This is all fiction.

Paperback ISBN: 978-1720153672
Hardback ISBN: 978-1951860219

As always:

To my beta-readers and "feedback crew": I am so glad you are all here. And I am so glad you are all so blunt with me—even if I do what I want most of the time.

To all of the readers: It has been quite a journey. I've loved every second of it. Let's get to the end together, shall we?

Also by Chase Connor

LGBTQ+ YA Books

Just a Dumb Surfer Dude: A Gay Coming-of-Age Tale
Just a Dumb Surfer Dude 2: For the Love of Logan
Just a Dumb Surfer Dude 3: Summer Hearts
Gavin's Big Gay Checklist
A Surplus of Light
The Guy Gets Teddy
GINJUH
When Words Grow Fangs

LGBTQ+ New Adult/Lit Fic/MM Romance

A Tremendous Amount of Normal
The Gravity of Nothing
Between Enzo & the Universe
A Straight Line (w/ co-author J.D. Wade)

LGBTQ+ YA & MG Fantasy

A Million Little Souls

A Point Worth LGBTQ Paranormal Romances

Jacob Michaels Is Tired (Book 1)
Jacob Michaels Is Not Crazy (Book 2)
Jacob Michaels Is Not Jacob Michaels (Book 3)
Jacob Michaels Is Not Here (Book 4)
Jacob Michaels Is Trouble (Book 5)
CARNAVAL (A Point Worth LGBTQ Paranormal Romance Story)
Jacob Michaels Is Dead (Book 6)
Jacob Michaels Is… The Omnibus Edition (all 6 JMI books and CARNAVAL)
Murder at the Red Rooster Tavern (Book 7)

Erotica

Bully
Briefly Buddies

Audiobooks

A Surplus of Light: A Gay Coming-of-Age Tale (narrated by Brian Lore Evans)
Between Enzo & the Universe (narrated by Brian Lore Evans; Tantor Media)

Translated

Between Enzo & the Universe – **Spanish**
A Surplus of Light – **Spanish**

Anthologies Contribution

Magis and Maniacs: And Other Christmas Stories (Frank, A Christmas in Pajamas, A Surfer's Christmas, and *The IT Guy)*

A Surplus of Light

Contents

Chapter 1

Ian

When the conditions are right, meaning that it is not too hot outside, and we've gotten enough rain, the creek fills all the way up. You can step right off of the bank and fall into the creek. The current is gentle and languid but moves at a quick enough pace to keep the water from becoming stagnant. But the creek is always full enough to at least get wet up to your waist. Crisp and cool, the water in the creek is a respite from the heat of late spring and early summer. A favorite hangout for all of the high school kids. Sometimes middle school kids will partake in the oasis that is the creek, but if the high school kids are around, they know to steer clear. It's just one of those unspoken rules kids have that no one really enforces, yet no one tries too hard to break.

Late at night is the best time to go to the creek, regardless of a person's age group. No one comes out to the creek late at night. Not because they're scared, but one of the major draws to swimming at the creek is that boys can check out girls and vice versa. You can't really do that in the dark. Early morning, just as the sun is coming up is a good time to go to the creek as well. Mostly because no one wants to get up at the butt crack of dawn during summer vacation. Even the added bonus of getting the creek all to oneself doesn't get most people out of bed so early.

Except for me.

I'm concerned neither with checking out girls nor am I worried about swimming in the dark of night. As long as I get to float lazily in the surprisingly crystal-clear water, enjoying the creek without the hoots and hollers of other kids, I could really care less about the time of day. When other kids are not around, I'm able to strip down to my swim trunks and wade out into the creek. You never jump in from the creek bed or cliff facings. The crystal-clear water makes it hard to determine the depth of the water in certain areas. And if you're all alone, you can't risk a broken appendage. Or worse.

Further down from where a lot of people usually swim, there's a wider and deeper stretch that can be leapt into without concern. However, I like the shallower area where I can lazily float and avoid the noise and boisterousness of other kids. Well, I couldn't really consider myself one of the "kids" anymore. High school was over for me and any friends that I had. Graduation ceremonies had been held a week prior. Everyone that had been seniors was in that strange limbo between where our old lives ended and where our new lives were going to begin.

We had a summer between phases of our lives, unsure of what we were really supposed to be doing as fresh-faced adults. Unsure if the colleges or jobs we had chosen were really the great escape we had been planning since middle school. For me, I didn't vacillate between worry and contentment. I was just ready. For what, I wasn't so sure—but I did know that escaping, no matter how that was achieved, was going to be fine. In a little over two months, Texas would be behind me and I would be heading to New York. Columbia was waiting. What happened after that, I didn't really care. I just wouldn't be in Texas anymore.

That's why I was floating in the creek at nearly midnight, only the moon for any light, staring up at the stars above. I was dreaming of the life that awaited me after my two-month lull between childhood and adulthood. The smile on my face reinforced my belief that I had made an excellent choice. Whether or not the students with who I had gone to school felt the same, or whether or not they had completely made up their minds about their futures, was of no concern to me. My path was set. First and foremost—wait, then leave. Escape. That's all that was required for me to begin being happy.

As I stared up at the stars in the cloudless sky, I mentally mapped out my future but found that my map ended at arriving at Columbia. After that, I had no solid plan for what my destination might be. It just wouldn't be the armpit of a town in Texas. When the stars were suddenly blotted out by a shoe, and then the sole of that shoe pressed itself against my forehead, my eyes grew wide in shock. Then I was being pushed under the water, no longer floating peacefully, but doing my best not to inhale water.

My arms flapped wildly, and I pushed my feet down, trying to find footing. My feet finally found purchase and I pushed my feet into the sandy bed of the creek, pushing upwards. The shoe was no longer pushing down on me, so I popped up out of the water with a gasp and a flinging of arms, water arcing wildly away from me as I sputtered and flapped like a floundering seal. I reached up and sluiced water away from my eyes, pushing my hair off of my face as I looked around angrily.

"You looked so peaceful." I looked directly in front of me towards the source of the voice.

Mike was sitting on the edge of the creek bank, his legs dangling beneath him, his feet just inches from the water's surface. He lit a cigarette dramatically, the orange glow cast by his lighter showing a wide shock of the white teeth that held his cigarette for a split second. He was amused. For a brief moment, I was tempted to send a wave of water towards him, putting out his cigarette and soaking him to the bone. But then I remembered how expensive cigarettes were and refrained.

"You're a fucking dick." I frowned at him.

Mike exhaled blue smoke into the darkness.

"You were wet anyway." The darkness that comprised his shoulders shrugged. "Stop being so dramatic."

I could hear the smile in his voice.

"I hope you choke on a cigarette." I waved a hand in front of my face, wafting the smoke away.

"So, what's up?" He grumbled. "You came out here without me?"

"Yeah? So?" I grumbled back and bent my knees until I was submerged to my neck so that I wouldn't get cold. "I always come out here at night."

"We always come out here at night," Mike replied before taking a long drag off of his cigarette.

His face was cast in a halo of orange, showing that he was smiling, and his eyes were twinkling.

"We're here aren't we?" I rolled my eyes, though I was sure he couldn't see my expression in the darkness.

Not until his eyes adjusted to the darkness, anyway.

"You still should have waited," he replied before he held out a pack in the dark. "You want one?"

"You know I don't want that shit." I scoffed playfully at the cigarette pack he held in his hand. "Cancer isn't really my thing, man."

He laughed throatily.

"You should really quit," I suggested. "I mean, school's over. Who's left to impress out here by the creek?"

"I don't smoke to impress people." He snorted.

"Right." I gave an upward nod. "I'm sure that you didn't take up smoking when you spied all of the half-naked bodies out here, man. I'm sure that had absolutely nothing to do with it. You're your own free-thinking person."

"I brought some weed if you prefer," he said.

"I'm not smoking that shit either," I replied. "You know, it's not fair that you have the 'All-American Boy' image and you're out here smoking and acting like you don't have the sense your momma and daddy could spare."

"And you got stuck with the 'troublemaker' image and you're out here acting like you got a stick up your ass."

"You're going to end up with a foot in your ass," I growled.

"Listen here, Columbia—"

"Get in the water and talk shit, Steedman." I stood suddenly, holding my arms out wide, water flying in all directions. "You wanna wrestle or what?"

Mike took a long drag on his cigarette, eyeing me quietly as I stood there, holding my arms out wide, aggressively. Several moments passed as we stared each other down in the darkness. Then our laughter pealed through the air before I fell back in the creek, sending streams of water slicing through the air around us. I laughed loudly up at the sky as I plunged back into the creek, water gushing up and around me, pulling me into its depths. Finally, I resurfaced and positioned myself so that only my head was sticking out.

The glow of Mike's cigarette was faint, signaling that he was almost done with the one and only cigarette he would smoke while he was out at the creek that night. I gave him a hard time—but he wasn't really a smoker. He had started smoking cigarettes to look cool, but now he just smoked one at night. Probably to calm his nerves. His own personal quiet time to settle his mind and slough off the stress of the day. I gave him shit, but I didn't really care. We all have our "thing," right?

"I'm going to miss this, man." Mike sighed as he tamped the cigarette out on the ground beside him.

"Don't talk like that," I said.

"When you're gone, what the hell am I supposed to do, Ian?" He sighed and tossed the butt over his shoulder into the darkness. "Everyone else around here sucks."

The way he drew out "sucks" was comical yet sad.

I stood and bowed grandly.

"I'm honored that you hold me in such high esteem." I laughed.

As I settled back into the water, Mike stripped his shirt off and laid it on the bank beside him.

"Serious, though, Ian," he said as he rose to his feet. "It's just not going to be the same here without you. Summers are always about us."

Mike and I never ran in the same circles in school. He was the All-American Boy, never in trouble, adored by all, the guy all girls wanted and never got, and the guy all other guys wanted to be. I was the smart kid with a penchant for making adults label me a troublemaker. Even though I did absolutely nothing to earn the title—usually—other than the aforementioned smart mouth—and a few fights. We never spent time with each other during the school year. And our social circles never overlapped. Actually, I didn't have much of a social circle, so overlapping never would have been an issue.

But during summers, our passions turned to our friendship. Neither of us liked swimming with the other kids in town, and we didn't care for pretending that we actually liked the friends we had made in school in order to survive. We had become a beacon of hope for each other. If we could just make it through the school year *one more year*, we could just be ourselves with each other. I didn't have to keep up my tough-guy exterior, and Mike didn't have to act like he enjoyed being popular and revered.

We could swim at night in the creek, spend time exploring the woods and the fields. Talk for hours about things that were actually important without others interrupting our flow or judging us. Talk about things that really interested us. Talk about politics and social movements. Discuss faraway places we hoped to travel to someday. Experiences we were dying to have. Foods we wanted to try but could never get in the Podunk town in which we were trapped. And neither of us judged the other. Ever.

Unlike other teenage guys, neither of us was just about sex, drugs, and rock n' roll. I mean, sex did come up quite a bit. And okay, so maybe Mike smoked weed from time to time, but it was by no means a habit. Honestly, I think he only kept it on himself so that he felt like he wasn't conforming to the All-American Boy image that had been cultivated and thrust upon him. I'd never actually seen him smoke weed. And, sure, we were teenage guys, so sex was at the forefront of our minds, but it wasn't the most important thing. Usually. We had more important things to talk about. Music was discussed, but it wasn't our main drive, either. We just liked talking about anything and everything we couldn't discuss with anyone else at school or home.

"Remember that first summer after eighth grade?" I could hear the smile in Mike's voice as he kicked off his shoes. "When I was totally convinced that you were as wild as your reputation made me believe?"

I laughed. "Yeah. Of course, I remember that."

Mike stripped off his jeans, leaving him in his swimsuit.

"You believed everything your dumbass friends told you." I continued. "I couldn't believe that I'd met someone my age that naïve."

"I couldn't believe I'd met such a badass." He countered as he shimmied down the bank into the water.

Mike sunk until he was underwater, stayed there for a moment, then rose back up to stand on his feet, the water coming to his waist. His hair was plastered against his skull and laying in a blondish seaweed-like curtain over his eyes as he smiled. Now that he was no longer in the shadows cast by the trees, but in the moonlight with me, I could see him better. The joy that was always affixed to his face was apparent in the moonlight, no longer hidden by the darkness that the tree cover provided.

Reaching over to him, I swiped my hand up his face and his forehead, brushing his hair back on top of his head. His eyes sparkled out at me, not their usual mossy green in the blue moonlight, but almost black. Mike smiled at me, his teeth looking blue from the light provided by the moon, but there was a sadness there as well. I smiled back, glad to have had such a good friend every summer during my high school years. Even if we were destined to go our separate ways in a few short months.

"Let me kiss you," Mike whispered.

"No, Mike." I used both of my hands to smooth his hair back.

"Just one."

"One leads to two," I said, moving my hands downwards once his hair was controlled. "Two leads to other things."

"I won't try other things."

"Because you're not going to kiss me." I ran my thumbs under his eyes, clearing away creek water.

Mike stared at me; his smile was now gone.

"You know," he whispered, "I would have loved you if you let me. I would have loved you for four years now."

"You already love me." I let my hands slide from his face, down his neck, to trace his collarbones with my fingers. "There's nothing about 'would have' in there, Mike. And that's why we shouldn't kiss."

"I would've been everything you wanted from me." He sighed as my fingers traced his chest. "I would have done anything. All you had to do was ask me to do it."

"I have nothing to give in return." I shrugged, my hands falling away from him, dipping into the water at my sides. "So, I'd never ask any of that of you, Mike."

"Why are you like this?" He leaned forward, his forehead touching mine, but he kept his lips away from mine.

He breathed out, sweet, soft, and warm against my mouth.

"It's just the way I am," I replied softly. "I've never lied to you about that, Mike."

Mike's hands came up to my shoulders and his hands squeezed them gently as he held his forehead against mine. The moonlight shone on the water around us, making the water look black and cold.

"You kiss me, then," he said.

"There are a lot of complications in a kiss," I replied.

"I want to be complicated," he said, his eyes boring into mine. "For once. I want us to be really complicated."

"No."

"You owe me a kiss. And I gave you four years like I promised." He smiled slightly. "You promised me that I would get another kiss from you...in the end. This feels like the end."

I pushed away from him gently.

"This isn't the end, Mike." I gave him the softest look I could manage. "It's just the end of me being here. Our friendship isn't over."

"It's as close to the end as we'll get while you're still here."

He stared at me for what felt like forever. The only sound being that of the slight breeze through the trees and the lapping of the water against the banks of the creek. Even though it was summer, the air was slightly cool. But I refused to shiver. I wouldn't show a hint of any type of weakness as I stood there before Mike. Even though he was the only person to who I could show my weaknesses, I refused.

"Everyone knows I'm bi, Ian," he said.

"I know."

"No one would care if you're gay."

"That's incorrect."

"Four years is a long time to only know who someone is during summer," Mike said.

"There's more daylight in summer," I replied. "It's a better time to see me."

He chuckled.

"And you know who I am," I said. "I've always been honest with you. You know me almost as well as I know myself."

"Just one kiss." Mike pleaded with me, falling to his knees in the water before me. "Give yourself to me like you said you would."

I waited for the water to settle.

"One?"

"Maybe two."

A mischievous grin bloomed, the blue light from the moon casting wicked, tempting shadows across his face. I looked down at him, less than four feet away from me, kneeling in the water. The moon smiled down at me, calling me a fool. The stars blinked in disbelief as I lowered myself to my knees, sinking into the water, but didn't move closer to Mike. I allowed myself to shiver slightly now that Mike could no longer see my body.

"Come and get it then." My voice was even, controlled.

Unemotional.

Uninterested.

Disguising.

"Do you want to kiss me?"

"No," I replied. "And yes."

"You know that I know I wouldn't be your first." Mike chewed at his bottom lip and looked down. "If, ya' know...you had let me love you."

"No," I replied. "You wouldn't be."

"You wouldn't be my first."

"I know that, too."

"I don't care." He looked up. "You know that, right?"

"Are you going to collect this kiss I owe you?" I asked.

"Only if you want me to." He smiled widely.

"We only play one game, Mike."

He looked down again, the wide smile disappearing into the shadows cast by the movement.

"If you want a kiss, you can have it," I said. "Come get it. But I'm not going to beg you or make this out to be something that it isn't."

"What is it?" His head snapped upwards.

"Me giving you what I promised."

"What if I don't want it now?"

"Stop it." I shook my head gently, my eyes not leaving his. "You want the kiss. I'll let you come get it. So, come get it."

"I hate you," he grumbled.

"No. You don't. I'd kiss you if you did." I sighed. "That's why this whole thing is a bad idea. But if you want complicated, come and get it. I have a lot of complicated over here."

Mike started to move in the water, sending ripples towards me before stopping himself.

"Will you still be my friend the rest of this summer?" He asked. "Our last?"

"Yes." I nodded.

Mike moved those few feet between us in the water and slowly raised his hands, curtains of water sliding off of his arms as he reached up to take my face between his hands. I raised my hands slightly to place one on either side of his hips as he pushed his body against mine. His eyes settled on mine and I returned his gaze as he looked at me contentedly.

"I love you," he whispered.

"Then kiss me," I whispered back.

So, he did.

Chapter 2

Mike
Summer Before Freshman Year

"*He's a fucking psycho, man,*" Kyle mumbled out of the corner of his mouth as we sat on the bank of the creek.

My question had been: "*Who is that?*"

I had been referring to the kid sitting on the other side of the creek, his back against a tree, his knees propping a sketchpad in front of himself as he worked with extraordinary focus. A dark swoop of hair hung in front of his face as his arm jerked quickly, his hand obviously flying over the pad of paper. He looked up every few seconds without moving his head. Other kids were sliding into the creek from the bank, jumping around in the water, splashing each other, screaming and laughing, acting like kids. But everyone stayed away from the kid by the tree. He didn't seem to notice.

"*Psycho?*" I frowned as I stared at the kid.

"*Yeah.*" Kyle snorted. "*He's like in a gang and shit. Apparently, he does drugs and has been arrested, like, a million times or something. You want one?*"

He held a pack of cigarettes out to me, one of the cigarettes sticking out of the hole he had torn in the foil.

"*Yeah.*" I shrugged as I pulled the cigarette free from the pack and put it behind my ear. "*Thanks, man.*"

Kyle shrugged as a form of acknowledgment and kicked his legs out in front of himself, leaning back to prop himself up with his hands. I stared at the kid as he sketched, though I had no idea what he was drawing. If it was even any good. I was enthralled. A real psycho. Someone that made Kyle, one of the toughest guys I knew, speak with fear, but also envy. The sound of the kids playing in the creek, running along the banks, and walking in from the woods, talking loudly to each other, slowly disappeared from my consciousness.

It was as if I were listening to see if I could hear any sound that the kid across the creek might make. Was he humming? Was he whispering to himself like a crazy person? What did his breathing sound like? Could I hear his art implement scratching on the paper? Everything around him seemed still and quiet, his own personal bubble. What did a vacuum sound like right there in the middle of chaos?

As if I found myself in a movie, the kid's head slowly rose, and his eyes connected with mine. My gut fluttered at the sight of his pale blue eyes, like icebergs floating in milk. They pierced into me and my gut flip-flopped, butterflies hopped up on caffeine. He stared back at me, impassively, his face a blank slate.

The face of a fallen angel.
Lips downturned like a bow.
Stuck between a frown and a smirk.
Kissable.
What?!
His hair hung in a curtain over his forehead, reaching to just below his eyebrows, but mercifully leaving his eyes unobstructed from view.
Skin that had known the sun, been kissed passionately by it.

Self-consciously, I looked down, lowering my head. I counted to ten. When I looked back up, he was staring back down at his sketch pad, his arm jerking furiously as he continued his work. I watched him for as long as I was brave, then forced myself to look away. Kids were dunking each other, laughing uproariously. I peeked at the kid. People were jumping into the creek, then rising to the surface and bellowing about banging their legs on the bottom. I peeked at the kid.

My gut flipped and flopped.

I felt giddy.

I peeked at the kid again.

"*I'm fucking thirsty.*" Kyle groaned dramatically next to me, then leapt to his feet. "*You wanna walk to the store with me? Then we can go hang out at my house or something?*"

"*Nah.*" I shook my head nonchalantly. "*I'm gonna chill here for a bit and then go home, man.*"

"*All right.*" He brushed off the seat of his shorts. "*See ya' tomorrow?*"

"*Yeah.*" I gave an upward nod.

Kyle walked away, grabbing our friend Dalton around the neck with a loud laugh. They walked off together through the woods, talking about getting something to drink. My eyes went back to the kid with the sketch pad. He looked up again, a vaguely irritated frown forming on his kissable mouth—*what?* —as his eyes met mine for the second time.

I looked away immediately, my stomach tightening and sending the butterflies into a flurry once again. Peering through the hair in my eyes, I looked up briefly, ever so slightly. The kid was standing and sliding his feet into his flip-flops. His sketchpad was tucked under one arm. Without looking over at me again, he walked away from the creek, in the opposite direction of the woods that Kyle and Dalton had gone. My breath caught in my throat and I instinctively found myself counting to twenty. Then I leapt up from my spot on the other side of the creek.

Exactly two minutes later, I found a shallow spot in the creek to dash across to the other side. I climbed up the bank and walked quickly towards where I had last seen the kid. Once I found the tree he had been sitting against, I walked in the direction that I had seen him go. I walked quickly to make up time between when he had left and when I had chased after him, but I didn't go so quickly as to seem eager if I ran into him.

The woods were plentiful on this side of the creek, littered with hills and cliffs, but there weren't as many vines and fallen branches and obstacles—save the hilly areas. I found myself walking up a steep hill, straining to climb in my flip-flops. When I crested the hill, I nearly gasped as I found myself at the edge of a cliff, just having avoided falling twenty feet to a trail below. I swallowed hard and exhaled slowly, silently, glad that I had avoided a broken leg—or worse—out in the middle of the woods.

Looking to my right down the pathway, I saw nothing but the trail and green trees. My head shot to the left, and a hundred feet away, I spotted the kid. He was sitting against a tree just off of the path, the sketchpad against his knees again as his arm worked furiously. I crouched down suddenly, trying to be silent as I stared at him sitting there and working on...whatever it was that he was drawing. The early summer breeze that blew down the trail ruffled his hair and tried to flip pages in his sketch pad.

I swore I could see a smile slide across his face as he patted the pages of his sketchpad back into place and tossed his head to get the hair out of his face. The kid worked peacefully and quietly, with purpose and focus. Within the bounds of a wild environment, he seemed to bring peace to the small space that he occupied. Chaos danced all around, but within his space, all was art and quiet purpose.

"Don't you walk away from me, fucker!" I jumped at the sound of a voice to the right on the trail.

I crouched down lower as my head snapped to the right. I looked over at the kid with the iceberg eyes. His head was raised, and he was peering off in the direction that the voice had come from as well. When I turned my head back to the right, I saw a kid— scrawny, short for his age—who I vaguely recognized as being in a few of my classes. He was walking quickly, his head down, looking afraid. Behind him, three kids—who I recognized as soon-to-be high school juniors—much larger than the kid from my class, followed.

"Hey!" The bully leading the others screamed at the kid. *"You better fuckin' stop!"*

I let my eyes slip over to the blue-eyed kid with the sketchpad. He seemed to let out a full-body sigh before he set his sketchpad down and rose to his feet. The small kid hurrying down the trail saw the kid by the tree and walked even more quickly in his direction. Stepping away from the tree, the kid who had been sketching waited until the kid was past him, then stepped into the trail, putting himself between the bullies and the bullied.

"Chambers." The lead bully laughed haughtily, and his friends joined in. *"Get the fuck out of my way."*

"There are younger guys to pick on that way, too." The kid, whose last name was obviously 'Chambers', nodded his head towards the other end of the trail. *"So, why don't you go that way?"*

"This has nothing to do with you." The bully seethed.

"Let's keep it that way," Chambers replied, bored.

The kid who'd had the bullies chasing after him was practically cowering a few feet behind Chambers.

"I'm not going to tell you again." The lead bully growled, his hands turning into fists at his side. *"Unless you want to get your ass kicked for this little faggot, you'll go back to drawing your little pictures."*

"Go away, Carson," The Chambers kid said, his voice still bland. *"You, too, Martin. Jon."*

Chambers was fearless. And I was in awe. My stomach was midnight at the dance club, again.

"I'm not going to tell you again." The lead bully, Carson, growled once more. *"If I have to kick your ass, I will."*

Chambers, who was several inches shorter than the three bullies, many pounds lighter, and obviously outnumbered, just stood there, staring impassively at Carson.

"Go swimming, Carson," Chambers said. *"Go to the store and get something to eat. Go home and play video games. This isn't something you have to do. No one will think any less of you if you walk away."*

My breath was caught in my throat. This kid wasn't taking the bait from this bully. He wasn't returning the insults and threats. He was being reasonable. And he seemed utterly bored with it all.

"One last time, Chambers!" Carson practically howled.

Chambers shook his head side-to-side in a way that was almost undetectable from my position so far away. Though, I doubted he had put much effort into the movement. The bullies didn't seem like the type he would waste much energy on.

Carson let out a howl of rage and the kid behind Chambers cowered even more, practically whimpering. Chambers stood there, his expression still bland and bored. Maybe sad. Carson ran towards Chambers and all I could think was: *Why did you have to get involved?* The sound of a fist connecting—a sharp crack of bone against flesh and deeper bone—made me jump. But Chambers was still standing, looking as bored and relaxed as before. Carson was on his back on the trail, laid out like the Vitruvian Man. I hadn't even seen the fist being thrown. Hadn't seen it connect. Chambers had clocked Carson so quickly and with such force, the fight was over before it even had a chance to begin.

Carson lay there limply for the most silent and tensest of seconds, everyone else frozen, waiting to see what would happen. Was Carson out cold or just stunned? *Was he dead??*

"*You broke my fucking nose!*" We all exhaled.

Except Chambers. His expression never changed.

"*It's not broken,*" Chambers responded. "*But you'll want to put ice on that eye.*"

"*You fucking piece of shit!*" Carson howled as he slowly sat up, his hand going to his eye. "*I'll fucking kill you!*"

Chambers took two steps to cross the distance between himself and Carson sitting on the trail. His steps were measured, even. Carson's friends jumped back. Chambers stood there before Carson, looking down at him, utterly and completely bored.

"*If you shut your mouth and leave now—that way—you can save some of your dignity.*" He spoke down at Carson. "*But I will hit you again if you force me. I don't want to fight you, Carson. But I will.*"

Carson held his face with one hand and glared up at Chambers with what could only be described as murderous disdain.

"*Why don't you two help him?*" Chambers looked at Jon and Martin.

Jon and Martin immediately grabbed Carson under his arms and pulled him to his feet. Chambers took a step back as Carson was brought to his feet. He was tough—but he wasn't dumb. Carson continued to glare at Chambers as his two friends drug him off in the opposite direction. Chambers returned the glare with a bored stare. But when the three bullies were around the bend and no longer in sight, Chambers turned to the kid who was standing a lot taller now that the fight was over.

"*You all right?*" He asked the kid.

"*Y-y-eah.*" The kid stuttered.

Not from fear. He had a stutter.

"*I told you not to come out here without your brother, Kevin.*" Chambers nudged him gently in the shoulder before going back to the tree. "*Guys like Carson are too scared to fuck with you when your brother is around.*"

"*I wuh-was juh-just walking home.*"

"*Stick to the streets, Kevin,*" Chambers said. "*Out here, Carson thinks he's king of the jungle or something.*"

Kevin laughed. "*I guh-guess you shuh-showed him, huh, Ian?*"

Ian Chambers.

That was his whole name.

Ian Chambers.

Righter of wrongs. Protector of the weak.

Brave.

Selfless.

Tough.

Kissable lips.

My stomach fluttered.

What was wrong with me?

"Buh-but you duh-didn't have to hit him so huh-hard."

"Some people don't understand mercy until they see mercilessness," Ian Chambers said, his head turning to Kevin. "Now...go home, Kevin. Tell your brother I said 'hi' for me."

"He duh-doesn't even like you," Kevin said.

"I know that." Ian Chambers smiled finally. "That's why you should tell him I said it."

Kevin chuckled nervously. He gave a small wave and dashed off in the direction he had been going before the fight. Ian Chambers watched Kevin running away for a moment, then turned back to the tree. He bent at his knees and scooped up his sketchpad. The sketchpad got shoved under his arm again, cradled against his side. I watched over the lip of the cliff as he stepped back onto the trail and turned in the direction that Kevin had run. He paused for a second, his back to me, and tilted his head upwards slightly.

"I'm going home now." He stated loudly. "There's no point in following me anymore."

I swallowed hard.

"Show's over." He added lowly, his voice sounding sad.

Ian Chambers didn't look back, didn't look directly at me, but I knew that he was speaking to me. Unless there was some other weirdo hiding in the woods, watching him teach a group of much older and bigger bullies a lesson. He walked with long, slow strides down the trail. The breeze blowing in his direction, as though patting him on the back. My heart was fluttering in my chest as my stomach started its dance party again.

Ian Chambers.

The name became my mantra. I found myself repeating it over and over in my head on the walk home. Over dinner with my family. In the shower. As I watched T.V. As I drifted off to sleep. That name and those lips, those iceberg eyes, that swoop of dark hair. A kid who could lay an older and bigger bully out with one punch but didn't actually want to fight. The kid who just wanted to sketch his pictures and be left alone. *Ian Chambers.* It might as well have been the name of a god.

For the next several days, I found myself looking for Ian Chambers everywhere I went—but especially when I went to the creek. Usually, it wasn't hard to spot him. He was always off to himself, sketching or simply laying against a tree, his eyes closed, a smile on his face as the sun shone down on him through the canopy of leaves. I'd find him at the creek almost every day, by his spot at the tree—a place none of the other kids tried to occupy. Ian Chambers wasn't a psycho after all.

Sometimes I'd have to walk to the trail where he had punched Carson to find him. He'd be sitting in the same spot by the tree, sketching in his pad, or just laid back against the tree, seemingly napping, but I knew that he was aware of everything going on around him. He could sense me there, watching him, trying to figure him out. Trying to muster up the courage to introduce myself and attempt to make him my new friend.

But he never opened his eyes when I watched him lay back with them closed. He never suddenly raised his head languidly to stare back at me. It was as if I ceased to exist to him. It was utterly frustrating and made my stomach flip and flop even more every time I watched him. Sometimes I'd find myself staring for minutes on end, not worrying about whether or not anyone else noticed my intent stares towards him.

A full week of summer went by where I stalked and stared, acted like I didn't have any sense or social skills. Finally, I realized that Ian Chambers was not going to speak to me unless he was spoken to directly. I had to make the move towards friendship if I wanted it. On a Sunday morning, when everyone was getting ready for church, I mustered up all of the courage I had and walked to the store. Using some of my allowance from the week, I bought two sodas and two bags of chips. I set out for the creek.

Ian Chambers was sitting in his same spot by the tree, but the creek was empty of any other kids. Everyone was going to church with their families. Then lunch—maybe by mid-afternoon there would be kids at the creek enjoying their summer away from school. But for now, this was Ian's personal sanctuary. I almost didn't approach him. But as I stood there, twenty feet away, the plastic bag from the store dangling at my side, Ian looked up and his eyes caught mine. He had been expecting me.

"*You still stalking me?*" He asked, then turned his attention back to his sketchpad. "*I thought you'd have given up by now.*"

He didn't talk like other kids who were about to start high school. He spoke like a world-weary adult. It matched his constantly bored facial expression.

"*What are you always drawing?*" I asked, giving him a wide berth as I walked toward him.

I walked toward him in an arc, not letting my eyes look at his sketchpad. That was too intimate. I didn't want to invade his vacuum. Gently, I sat down a few feet away, giving him plenty of room as he pulled his hand away from the sketchpad.

"*Usually trees,*" he said simply, those blue eyes coming to rest on mine. "*Sometimes other kids. Birds. That squirrel there.*"

He motioned with his head. I looked in the direction he had nodded and had seen a squirrel laid out on a large rock behind me. My eyes grew wide, taking in the stillness and quiet of the squirrel.

"*Is he dead?*" I whispered.

Ian made a sudden, high-pitched squealing noise. The squirrel jumped up quickly onto its hindquarters, its head whipping back and forth. It looked at Ian quickly, then me, then it dashed away so quickly it was a blur.

"*He was just sunning himself,*" Ian said.

I gave a relieved chuckle then turned my attention back to Ian.

"*What have you got there?*" Ian nodded at the bag.

"*I, uh, I brought us some sodas and chips,*" I replied shyly. "*If you want some, anyway.*"

"*I don't eat,*" Ian said.

I frowned at him.

"*Or drink.*" He continued. "*I consume the blood of virgins and smoke the reefer and I joined a gang right before school last year. Sometimes you can see me swimming in the creek at night, worshipping Satan.*"

I stared at him for a long time.

"*Is any of that true?*" I asked lowly.

He stared back for an even longer time, considering me. The silence hung between us as he leveled me with his eyes.

"*I like swimming at night.*" He nodded. "*But I don't believe in Satan. And it's kind of hard to find a virgin nowadays.*"

I gave a nervous chuckle.

"*Why does everyone say those things about you?*"

"Carson, the guy you saw me with the other day?"
I nodded.

"That's not the first time I've had to punch him," Ian replied, his eyes sad. *"After the first time, he started making up stories about me. He didn't realize that it made no difference to me."*

"I guess he never learns." I smiled sheepishly.

"I don't like hurting people. No matter what you might have heard."

I glanced at his knuckles. They were covered in old, dark bruises.

"I believe you." I breathed out, my stomach flipping around.

Ian watched me for a moment, then closed his sketchpad and stretched his legs out, letting the sketchpad lay in his lap.

"So, what kind of chips and soda did you bring?" He smiled.

"I, uh, didn't know what you'd like, so," I opened the bag and pulled out my purchases, *"I just got two Cokes and a couple of bags of Cheetos."*

"Perfect," he said. *"But I don't have any money."*

"It's cool." I tried to cover up my pride at responding so casually. *"I had some allowance saved up."*

Ian Chambers stared at me for a moment, then flipped his sketchpad open, flipping through pages casually before stopping. He deftly ripped one of the pages out and held it out to me.

"We're even," he said simply.

My eyes stayed on his as I took the paper from him. I didn't look away from him until the paper was in front of me. Ian Chambers had sketched me. Sitting on the other side of the bank on the day that

I had first laid eyes on him. He had probably done it from memory. It was remarkable.

"*Wow.*" I breathed the word.

"*It's not my best.*" Ian rose to his knees so that he could grab his Coke and bag of Cheetos. His fingertips were charcoal black. *"But it's not my worst."*

"*It's...amazing.*" I looked up at him with a smile.

"*Thank you,*" he replied, twisting the cap of his soda as he sat back down. *"I like your hair. You should let it grow out even more."*

The butterflies in my stomach rejoiced. My cheeks flushed.

"*So...what's your name?*" I asked him.

Ian cocked an eyebrow at me.

"*Okay.*" I blushed deeper.

"*And you're Michael Steedman.*"

"*Mike. I go by 'Mike' to everyone but my mom,*" I replied.

"*What does your mom call you, Mike?*" He grinned as he brought the Coke to his glorious lips and took a sip.

"*Sugar Man,* mostly." I blushed so deeply that I could feel the heat of my own face.

Ian continued to grin. But he didn't laugh.

"*You look like a 'baby boy' or 'junior' to me, personally,*" he replied. "*Sugar Man doesn't really fit you.*"

I laughed gently, grateful that he hadn't teased me.

"*But there are worse things than 'Sugar Man', I guess.*" He shrugged.

"*Do you want to be my friend?*" I spat it out.

I cursed myself for being such a dork. Ian's grin disappeared. We were staring at each other again.

"*All right.*" He nodded.

"*Good.*" I smiled and reached for my bag of Cheetos.

Chapter 3

Mike
Later That Summer

"*Will you teach me to fight?*" I asked without moving my lips too much. "*Please?*"

"*No,*" Ian answered. "*Stop moving.*"

"*I'm not moving,*" I mumbled.

He growled playfully at me as I sat there. I smiled internally but fixed my face and kept staring straight ahead—as I had been for far too long. The last bit of summer sun pierced through the trees and cast circles and squares of yellow light on everything around us. Everything was dry and crisp, the ground hard and crumbly. The grass was like hay. Summer was ending and this was our last Saturday before we had to return to school.

All summer long, Ian and I had been inseparable. Day after day we had spent together, one adventure after another. At night, for as long as we were allowed, we sat outside of my house, talking, laughing, whispering secrets like we were girls. When I had told Ian that we were whispering like girls, he had frowned and said: "*Girls aren't the only humans who want to keep their secrets.*" I had taken that to heart. I no longer intimated such things again.

Girls aren't sluts and whores just because they like sex. They're sexually liberated. Women aren't bitches because they're confident and aggressive. Ian corrected me when I got confused about those things.

Ian taught me how to sneak into the movies. How to approach animals in the woods so as to not startle them away. How to hold and flex one's hand so that a nearby butterfly might alight. How laying on top of a round hay bale under the moon felt like you were staring out into the universe as the sweet smell of bundled, dried grass tickled your nose. He taught me how to talk to people in a way that honored them in the way that a person ought to be. He taught me to respect everyone. Even if they didn't respect you.

He taught me how to look a person in the eyes, no matter how big and bold they were, and tell them the truth. Even when they didn't want to hear it. I also learned that he absolutely hated Cokes and Cheetos. He preferred iced tea mixed with lemonade and dill pickle sunflower seeds. Which he taught me to shell using just my teeth and tongue and to spit the shells so far you'd never find them. He showed me all of the lesser-traveled trails in the woods. Where the best parts to swim in the creek were. How to stand up for myself. How to be a good friend.

When he wasn't paying attention—which wasn't often, since he seemed to be hyper-aware of everything around him—I'd stare at his lips. His eyes. Study his profile. Let my stomach dance joyfully within my belly. Once or twice, he'd turn and catch me staring at him, smiling like a puppy dog. After a few times of catching me, he started returning to the position he was in and hold it. He'd let me study him for as long as I liked. He never said anything about it. Never teased me.

Summer had always been the best part of the year, but now I had a love affair with the season. The days were long, and the sun hung heavily in the sky for a length of time that was never long enough each day. Those minutes and hours were filled with an irrevocable obsession with my new friend. The best friend I'd ever had. I could just be me. Ian let me just be me.

"*How long does this take?*" I mumbled again.

"*I'm almost done, but it'll take longer if you don't stop moving.*" He hissed at me, a smile on his face as he concentrated. *"You're the one who wanted this, so suck it up."*

I smiled but quickly affixed the blank look back on my face.

A few minutes later and Ian's hand dropped from his sketchpad.

"Okay." He sighed. *"We're done."*

I rolled my neck and wiggled my limbs, my muscles and joints sore from sitting in the same position for so long. Ian held his sketchpad out to me. I reached out and took it from him, once again looking him in the eyes as I accepted his offering. When the sketchpad was before me, I looked down. It was the most beautiful drawing that I'd ever seen. It was a real portrait of me—not one that he had sketched from memory. He had captured the minuscule bump on the ridge of my nose. The freckles that always decorated my cheeks at the end of summer. The way my hair had grown out, golden and down to my ears. The way one side of my mouth was always upturned.

"It's...it's amazing, Ian." I breathed out.

"Thank you," he replied evenly. *"It's all yours."*

"Really?" I grinned down at the picture.

"Si, senor," he replied. *"For being such a good friend all summer."*

I looked up at my new best friend—the best friend I'd ever had, holding the sketchpad tightly in my hands. I wanted to tell him that it was he who had been the best part of my summer. It was he who had made the whole season as glorious as it had been. That my life was made immeasurably better just by becoming his friend. That I had never had such a great two-and-a-half months in my entire life. That when it rose each day, I was invigorated with all the light of the sun, knowing that I was going to see him again. But I didn't have the words at that age.

"*It's the nicest thing anyone has ever given me,*" I said, basically to no one and everyone.

"*I'm glad you like it.*" The corner of his mouth turned up.

"*I do.*" I nodded. "*You're crazy talented, Ian.*"

He shrugged. "*I could be better. I'm taking art for my freshmen elective.*"

"*I'm taking Public Speaking.*" I frowned. "*Getting that out of the way.*"

He laughed.

"*I think I'll wait 'til sophomore year for that.*" He shrugged again.

"*Maybe we'll have some classes together?*"

"*Maybe.*"

Ian stretched out and laid back in the dry grass under the tree, his skin shiny with perspiration. He folded his hands behind his head and closed his eyes as he smiled to himself. Gently, I crawled up beside him and laid down, mimicking his positioning and posture. But I didn't close my eyes. I turned my head to stare at him, taking in the curves and angles of his profile. Butterflies had lived in my stomach all summer. I was starting to understand what that meant. But it didn't unnerve me. It felt like a final piece to the puzzle of who I was had been dropped into place.

"*This has been the best summer of my life,*" I said softly.

"*All fifteen years of it.*" He chuckled, his eyes staying shut.

"*Exactly.*" I chuckled with him.

I rolled to my side, propping myself up on my elbow as I stared at my best friend. He continued to lay there, his forehead, upper lip, and torso shiny with sweat. Something in my inexperienced teenage gut leapt. I didn't quite understand it at that age, but I knew that I liked it. That I wanted that feeling to be what I felt all day every day.

"*I hate that summer's over,*" I said simply.

"*It's not quite over.*" He grinned, his eyes still closed.

"*May as well be.*" I sighed.

Ian's eyes flicked open before I could move my gaze from his stomach.

I blushed.

"*Are you gay?*" He asked.

"*Wh-what?*" I sputtered.

"*It's a pretty simple, innocent question.*"

"*Why would you think that I'm gay?*"

"*It's just a question, Mike.*"

"*I like girls,*" I answered quickly.

Ian stared at me for a very long time. He stared until I was uncomfortable and wondering if his near-lethal fist would strike out if he suspected that I was gay. Suddenly, he just nodded. He laid back in the grass, his hands under the back of his head.

"*I suppose that's an answer,*" he said simply.

I swallowed hard.

"*You can stare all you want.*" He sighed, stretching his body languorously. "*It's just us here.*"

"*You...you don't care?*" I whispered, wary.

"*No, Mike.*" He opened his eyes briefly to look at me. "*It doesn't bother me in the slightest.*"

"*Okay,*" I replied gently.

So, I stared. I took in the way that the beads of sweat shone on his forehead, the way his forehead dipped down to the bridge of his nose, then back up to his button nose. The prominent dimple on his left cheek when he smiled. His kissable lips. His dark hair that hung toward the grass around his head. His chest, rising and falling with each breath, beaded with sweat. The way his rib cage led to his abdomen and the way his stomach looked concave as he laid there on his back, his lower ribs poking out with each breath. My best friend made my stomach dance.

We stayed like that for a very long time. Ian's eyes stayed closed, respectful and permissive of this private time that my eyes had with his body. My best friend knew that I was drawn to him in this way, but he didn't care. He wasn't threatened or offended—just curious about it. And he didn't care if I appreciated his body. He was an artist. He had probably stared at people like that before, too. What went on in his head while he stared could have been the same as what went on inside of mine, but he wasn't giving that information.

"Don't you think you should get home to eat?" Ian spoke, his eyes still closed.

I looked up, realizing that the sun was dipping close to the horizon.

I sputtered for a moment.

"Um, yeah," I said finally. *"Mom probably has dinner ready."*

He opened his eyes and propped himself up with his elbows.

I stood from my spot beside him and started to walk away.

"You...you won't say anything to anyone, will you?" I turned my head slightly. *"Please?"*

"It never would have crossed my mind, Mike," he replied.

"Okay." I breathed out slowly.

"What are you doing tonight?" He asked, making no effort to move.

"Um, nothing I guess." I didn't want to turn back. I was in no condition to do that.

"Meet me at the creek?" He suggested. *"One last swim before school starts? Midnight?"*

"I don't know if I can sneak out that late." My stomach was fluttering again.

"I'll see you at midnight then, Mike." I could hear the grin in his voice.

That was the first time that I felt hate for my best friend. Well, not real hate. But I wanted to hate him. Because he knew me as well as I knew myself. I would sneak out of the house at midnight—no matter the consequence. Because I wouldn't miss an opportunity to have one last swim with my friend. And he'd never invited me to swim at night with him before. I had been dying for him to invite me out to the creek at night. And he knew that.

God, I wanted to hate him.

But my stomach just fluttered instead.

So, at midnight that night, my swimsuit put on under my jeans, and a t-shirt pulled on over my head, I scurried out of my bedroom window, silent as I could be. There was no moon to speak of and everything was quiet in my neighborhood. The whole town was dead. Which was never unusual for such a small town on a Saturday night. I ducked between houses, scurried down streets like a bandit, and made my way to the woods.

Feeling my way carefully through the dark of the woods, I did my best to not fall and break my leg as I made my way to the creek mostly by memory. When I approached the creek, the swath that it cut through the woods was a haven of blue light, where some of the light cast by the moon and stars could actually pierce through the canopy. I could see Ian's dark figure standing on the bank of the creek, waiting for me. The smile that bloomed on my face was immediate and painful. I felt like my face would split.

When I got closer to Ian, his head turned ever so slightly at the sound of my approach. He smiled, the white of his teeth and his eye caught that blue light. He was already stripped down to his swimsuit. A warm breeze blew through the path that the creek cut through the woods and his hair was ruffled, falling into his eyes. He reached up and pushed it back gracefully as I came to stand beside him.

"*Took you long enough,*" he said.

"*I left my house right at midnight to be sure I wouldn't get caught,*" I whispered.

"*There's no one here to hear us, Mike.*" He chuckled.

"*Right.*" I cleared my throat.

"*I want you to see something,*" he said. "*Come on.*"

"*Okay.*"

I expected him to lead me into the woods or further along the creek. Instead, he shimmied down into the creek. I shrugged and followed him down into the water. It was still warm from the sun beating down on it all day long. Ian slowly eased himself under the water. I followed his lead and dunked myself under. We both rose out of the water at the same time, our hair plastered to our heads. In unison, we pushed our hair back on our heads. Ian smiled at me, then held a finger to his lips.

"*Stay very still.*"

I didn't answer but stayed as still as possible.

We were quiet and still for a very long time.

"*There,*" Ian whispered and pointed.

Something black swooped from a tree on one side of the creek, down to the water, then back up into a tree on the other side of the creek. Then another black thing. Then another. Then another. Dozens of these black things swooped down and nearly flew into the water, but rose right before, back into the trees.

"*What are those?*" I whispered.

"*Mexican Free-Tailed Bats.*" He chuckled lowly.

I froze.

"*They won't hurt us,*" he whispered. "*They're catching bugs—their dinner.*"

I became a little less tense.

"*This is the best time to see them. Pretty soon, they'll be migrating back to Mexico for the winter,*" he whispered. "*Right now, the pups are learning to hunt and forage and take care of themselves.*"

I watched the bats for several minutes, standing still in the water so as to not disturb the surface. Ian smiled up at the bats as they swooped down to catch bugs at the water's surface. My fear of the bats quickly abated, and I found myself smiling each time another bat swooped down, inky black in the darkness, then swooped back up. Some looked as big as birds, others were relatively tiny. Those must have been the "pups."

"*It's kind of beautiful,*" I whispered.

Ian nodded.

"*Is this why you come out here at night?*"

"*No,*" Ian whispered back. "*You can only guarantee that you'll see the bats in late August. I just come here for peace and quiet.*"

"*I'm here.*"

"*You don't bother me so much.*" He turned his head slowly to smile at me.

Against all instinct, all nature or nurture, I found my hand sliding slowly through the water to Ian's. He looked down, surprised as I grabbed his hand. Then he looked over at me. His eyes looked black in the dark as they met mine. But as my fingers slid between his, he accepted my hand. We stared at each other for a very long time, then turned our attention back to the bats, our hands still together. The bats fed for several minutes. And it was the most glorious and exhilarating minutes of my life up until that moment.

After several minutes, the appearance of the bats got further and further apart, until it was apparent that they were done for the night. I turned to my best friend, took his face in my hands, and pressed my lips against his. He stood there passively as my lips pressed amateurishly against his, our bodies against each other's. It was the most titillating experience of my life. When I felt Ian's hand slide up and press against my chest, something in my head said: *"This is it."*

But then he gently pushed me away, separating our lips.

"I'm sorry." Is what came out of my mouth, but my body tried moving towards his again.

"Whoa." He smiled at me, holding his hand against my chest.

The strength he mustered up with ease let me know how hard he must have been able to punch when he had to. Carson's eye had been black for two weeks. I never would have been able to push past that arm unless he willed it. That, too, was arousing.

"I think you've had enough of bats." He teased.

"I'm sorry," I said again.

"*Don't be sorry,*" he said, his hand still on my chest.

"*Did you...did you like it?*" I looked down.

"*You're a fair to good kisser, Mike,*" he said. "*But I won't do this with you. I won't do that to you.*"

"*Won't—or don't want to?*" I asked, looking up.

"*Won't,*" he replied simply. "*I'm...I'm...*"

He took a long time trying to find the right words—which was unnerving. Ian always had the most perfect words.

"*I'm your best friend.*"

"*That doesn't sound like it's what you wanted to say.*"

"*It isn't.*" He agreed. "*But it's what I'm going to say. For now.*"

"*Will you kiss me again?*" I asked gently. "*Before the end?*"

"*What does that mean?*" He frowned.

"*Before you decide you don't want to be my friend anymore.*"

"*Why would I decide to stop being your friend?*" He laughed like it was the most ridiculous thing he'd ever heard.

I shrugged. I shivered.

Ian considered me for a moment.

"*Yes,*" he said. "*I'll kiss you again before the end.*"

We got out of the creek after a quick swim, dried off as best we could, pulled our clothes on, and walked through the woods in silence. When we got to the edge of the woods, Ian took my hand in his again, lacing our fingers together, and looked into my eyes for several minutes. Then he let go and headed off in one direction while I headed in the other. I only looked back a few dozen times, watching his figure cut through the dark.

I didn't see Ian all Sunday. Even though I went to the store, to the creek, to the field where we laid on top of hay bales, our special places in the woods. He was nowhere to be found. And I had no idea where he lived, so I couldn't just stop by and knock on a door. He had never given me a phone number, which in and of itself was weird. But, while I was internally panicking, I knew that I'd see him in school, so I swallowed my panic.

When Monday came, and I walked into high school for the first time with my friends, I was overwhelmed. In a good way. I was a high school student—and I had the cool friends. And I had a best friend who was even cooler than all of them—even if he wasn't the psycho that they had labeled him. Ten minutes before the first bell, Ian walked in the front doors as I was closing my locker. There was nothing in it yet, but I had just been making sure that I remembered my combination given to me at orientation.

Ian walked through the main hall, other kids going out of their way to make a path for him. He stared straight ahead, not seeming to notice the effect he had on the other students. Indifferent to the stares and whispers and wide-gaped mouth looks. When he got closer, I smiled widely and raised my hand in a wave. Ian looked over at me blankly, as if he didn't know who I was. And then he was gone. His lip had been split. *His perfect lip.*

I only ever saw my...*best friend?*...at lunchtime my whole freshmen year. We didn't have a single class together. Apparently, he was in the advanced placement classes. He didn't take any "regular" classes with the rest of the "normal" students. And he always sat at the end of some lunch table, as far away from anyone else that he could. Sometimes, Kevin, the kid he had protected in the woods would sit down with him. Ian didn't talk to him much, but Kevin talked to Ian a lot. After a few minutes, Kevin's older brother would come and pull him away from the table. He'd speak angrily to Ian for a second while Ian just stared at him impassively.

Once Kevin and his brother were gone, Ian would just go back to eating his lunch. At least every other week, Ian would come to school with a split lip, or a bruise, or red eyes. But he never said a word to anyone unless forced. He stared straight ahead and went from one class to another, to his locker, to lunch, as if there were no other students around. When Kevin tried to talk to him at lunch, Ian would do his best to ignore him. Until Kevin's brother came and pulled him away again. After a few months, Kevin's brother stopped being angry with Ian and wouldn't speak to him, but he still wouldn't let Kevin sit with Ian.

A few times I had found myself leaving the lunch line, drawn to the half-empty end of the table Ian was stationed at with no one to talk to. When he'd see me approaching, he'd look up at me with a blank stare. He'd stop chewing his food and just stare until I lost my resolve and went to the table I usually sat at with my friends. I began to hate my friend. Not real hate. But he wouldn't talk to me or even look at me unless it was to run me off. And I never saw him outside of school for the entire school year.

Chapter 4

Ian

. My hands rested on Mike's hips as he kissed me deeply, passionately, four years of unexpressed passion bleeding into my mouth. I kissed him back, doing my part in this activity that meant so much to him. To our friendship. I wanted to melt into his body, to feel myself push against him like he pushed against me. Instead, I kept my hands on his hips and returned his kiss as controlled and measured as I could manage. Mike's hands went from my face, down to my neck, then around to my shoulders. Then they were sliding lower, and he was cupping my ass.

That was the furthest I'd let him go since we'd met.

"You said you wouldn't try other things." I pulled my face away gently.

It was ironic, considering what I felt poking against my stomach.

"Please?" He whispered.

I returned my mouth to his, picking up where we left off. His tongue rolled into my mouth and I accepted it, let my tongue mingle with his as an involuntary moan escaped his throat. His hands were squeezing my ass and his mouth seemed to be feeding upon me. His groin was straining against the front of his swimsuit and jabbing me in the stomach. Then his hands were rising to the small of my back and his fingers began to snake their way into the waistband of my swimsuit.

"Okay, handsy." I pushed away gently, putting a few inches between us.

It wasn't nearly enough space.

"I said 'please.'" He grinned evilly at me. "And you acquiesced."

"Someone learned something studying for his SATs." I teased, my hand against his chest.

"I just listen to you talk," he replied.

I started to pull away.

"Don't." Mike pleaded as he grabbed my hand and held it against him.

"Mike..."

"Just tonight, Ian." He closed his eyes as his face twisted up in longing. "Just let me have tonight. *Please.*"

"What does that mean?"

"Just be with me."

"*I'd kind of like to know what that entails.*" That's what I meant to say. Instead, I said: "Okay."

Then Mike's mouth was back on mine, invading mine with his tongue and his hands were sliding down the back of my swimsuit. The flesh of his hands connected with the flesh of my ass and he pushed his groin into my stomach as we knelt in the water and kissed. My hand wandered from his chest down to his stomach, then both of my hands were on his stomach, exploring the soft flesh there, before moving around to his back.

"*Lower.*" Mike breathed against my mouth before kissing me more.

I *acquiesced* and lowered my hands, running them over the mounds of Mike's ass, cupping him in my hands, pulling his groin into my stomach forcefully. He groaned against my mouth, his hands squeezing my ass as he did his best to drink me in. Then his hands were moving around to the front of my swimsuit and his fingers began pulling at the front waistband. When I pulled away this time, it was more forceful, and I backed up more than a few inches.

"Don't." Mike pleaded.

"Let's just calm down for a minute," I said, controlling my voice. "Or several."

"I'm not trying to force you into anything, Ian," he said.

"You couldn't," I replied instinctively.

"I know that, Ian." He nodded. "But you know what I meant."

I nodded back after a moment.

"I just wish you'd stop fighting against me." He sighed. "You can posture and pose any way you want, but there's no reason to hold back anymore. Let's just have this one night. You'll be gone in a few months anyway."

"There's the crux of the problem."

"If I'm willing to get my heart broken, the least you can do is agree to be the one who breaks it," he replied.

I really had no response for that. Mike wasn't a fifteen-year-old kid who thought that the world around him was the same as the world he knew at home. He'd learned things. He knew things. He had witnessed things. He was no longer innocent and bright-eyed and unable to understand how ugly the world could be. He knew why I was the way that I was—even if he acted like he didn't understand.

If he wanted his heart broken, who was I to deny him? I was his best friend, that was who I was. If I broke his heart, it might be the last shred of goodness I had left in my heart that would be sloughed away. Mike might survive, but I wasn't so sure that I would. That's what made me put my hand against his chest to push him away, time after time. That's what made me control myself around him. It wasn't fear of what it might do to him—it was fear of whether or not it would be the end of me.

"*You are unbearable.*" I hissed.

"This is your fifth summer being my best friend." He smiled. "I think one more night won't be impossible for you to endure me."

"I don't endure you, you jerk." I sunk neck-deep in the water.

"Then...what do you do?"

He moved inches closer but was cautious this time.

"I count down school days." I hissed at him again. "I endure whispers and stares and angry shouts and fists thrown and legs kicked out. I endure being the only person who stands up to the jerks of this fucking town. I endure split lips and black eyes. *I endure...*I endure a lot of things—but you're not one of them."

Mike didn't move closer.

"I haven't seen a bruise on you since right after school started," Mike whispered. "And that was just your knuckles."

"I resolved that situation." I glared at him.

"I know. Do you want to talk about it?" Mike asked.

"No." I snapped. "I don't."

Mike paused. But just briefly.

"I know that you know that I know about that," he whispered.

"Everyone knows, Mike." I couldn't help but let a bitter laugh escape my throat. "That doesn't make you special."

"What makes me special is that I think I was the last to know." Mike didn't react to my anger. "You didn't care who knew. Except me. You tried to protect me from that."

I just glared at him.

"I know that you *resolved* that situation." Mike continued. "I was there that night. Like I wish I'd been every night."

"I know you were." I sighed. "But I figured if you were still playing dumb, I would, too."

Mike smiled pitifully at me.

"Everyone in this town may as well have been there. Every single night." I spat. "Because everyone knew. And no one cared. They were happier making stories up about me than facing the truth. Rather than doing the right thing. I was just one kid with a problem that was too...*messy*...to deal with. Easy to ignore. Easy to pretend that everything was fine. So...if you want me tonight...you can have me. 'Cause that's all I have left in me. And if I'm going to give the last of myself to someone—it should be you."

"I don't want you to give yourself to me, Ian." Mike was in front of me now. "I want you to share yourself with me."

"It is summer." I clenched my teeth.

"It always has the most light." He laid his forehead against mine.

I sighed. "The best time to see me."

"I see all of you all of the time," Mike whispered against my mouth. "Even here. Right now. In the dark."

I didn't move away.

"I saw you every day in the hallways at school. Sitting at the lunch table alone. Ignoring Kevin. Not standing up and punching his brother in the face, no matter what insult he hurled at you. I saw you hold your head up against all of the stares and whispers and insults hurled your way, not giving a shit the whole way."

"I gave quite a few shits, actually."

"Well, you didn't let them know that." He smiled against my mouth. "You were a tough bastard all through high school. Never once did anyone do or say anything to you that made you lose control. But you stood up for others...even when they didn't deserve it. You won."

"Winning doesn't matter if you're broken afterward," I replied.

"You're not broken," he said. "At least, not for long."

"Are you trying to finish putting me back together?" I pulled my face back to glare at him. "Is that what this is about tonight?"

Mike grabbed my head and pulled me into him, kissing me tenderly on the lips. I let him.

"It's about letting you know that someone would have cared," he whispered as he pulled back from my mouth. "If you had just let him."

I stared at him.

"I want to care about you for as long as you'll let me." He added.

"I want to get out of the water," I replied.

"You're not leaving, are you?" He frowned.

"No," I said. "I just want to be dry for a bit."

So, we got out of the water. We shimmied back up the bank and sat down side by side, our hips touching with our knees pulled up and our arms wrapped around them. And we stared up at the canopy of the trees.

Chapter 5

Mike
The Beginning of Another Summer

I wasn't going to search him out. I just wasn't. He didn't deserve my friendship. I was pacing the floor of my bedroom. I had just gotten home from my last day of freshman year. I wouldn't go to the creek. I wouldn't go to the field where the hay bales would be later in the season. I wouldn't go to the store. I wouldn't go to the numerous places that were ours in the woods. Even as I paced the floor angrily, I was stripping out of my school clothes and pulling on basketball shorts and a t-shirt. I knew that I was going to find him.

When I exited my house, headed towards the creek, I was angry still. My feet slammed into the sidewalk in front of my house and on the asphalt of my street. First, I went to the store. He was nowhere in sight. I marched all the way to the woods, through the woods, and to the creek. A few kids had shown up to celebrate the end of the school year, but no Ian. I crossed the creek at its shallowest point and headed to the trail.

And there he was. Sitting back against the tree he always sat at, his knees propping his sketchpad in front of himself. I stood on the cliff overlooking the trail, waiting for him to look up, but he never did. Angrily, I stomped down the path that led from the top of the cliff to the trail below. My feet slammed into the earth over and over again as I got closer to Ian. When I was within ten feet of him, he spoke.

"*It's really best if you don't try to be my friend at school,*" he said, his hand still moving over the skctchpad. "*You have enough things to worry about without defending your friendship with me, Mike.*"

"*Fuck you.*" I groaned.

"*I'm giving free advice here.*"

"*You couldn't have told me, like, last summer, or pulled me aside at school...or something?*" I growled. "*You just ignored me for nine months, like you were ashamed of being my friend?*"

"*Is that what you thought?*" He looked up but his hand didn't leave the pad. "*That you kissed me, and I was afraid we'd be labeled homos together? Or that I thought you were a nasty queer?*"

"*Are you trying to be hurtful?*"

"*No. Trying to make a point,*" he said. "*That you assumed that there was underlying shame or embarrassment at being your friend. If you are my friend at school, you have a target on your back, too.*"

"*What does that have to do with anything, asshole?*" I spat.

He stared at me for a very long time. A breeze blew down the trail, ruffling the pages in his sketchpad. He didn't try to hold them in place. He let them flutter in the breeze as he stared up at me. The silence was becoming unbearable. And I was losing my resolve.

"*My brother had a drug problem,*" he said. "*And my dad is an alcoholic. And my mother left a long time ago. Well, not physically.*"

"*What does that have to do with you?*"

"*My brother screwed people over,*" he said. "*He stole. He cheated. He killed two kids in a car wreck.*"

"*I don't remember hearing anything about that.*"

"*He was ten years older than us,*" he said. "*Everyone assumes that I'm just like him. And due to my dad's escapades here in town—and, well, anywhere he goes, that just makes them think I'm probably doing drugs and drinking. I'm a 'bad kid', Mike. I'm trash and shouldn't be allowed to hang out with other people's kids.*"

"*No, you aren't.*"

"Truth doesn't matter." He shrugged. *"But there you have it. If you're my friend, you're probably like me. So, keep your distance at school. That's why Kevin shouldn't be my friend—and why his brother won't let him be friends with me."*

"Where's your brother now?"

"Dead."

"Oh." I looked away. *"The car wreck?"*

"No," he replied evenly. *"He OD'd a year later. I loved my brother. A lot. But...he was an imperfect human being. And I don't think he ever had any remorse for his abhorrent behavior. Ever."*

"Where's your dad?"

"Right now?" He asked. *"The Gulf."*

I rolled my eyes and went to sit in front of my friend.

"Why didn't you just tell me? Prepare me for being ignored all year?"

"I still wasn't sure that you were really my friend," he said. *"But here you are. So, now I'm telling you."*

"You can tell me anything," I growled at him. *"Anytime."*

"Okay." He nodded.

I sat in front of him for a moment, looking into those pools of milk with the floating icebergs, and all of my anger disappeared.

"So...are we going to kiss and make up?" I tested the waters with a grin.

He grinned and rolled his eyes.

"That's really the best you could come up with?" He laughed.

I shrugged. *"Worth a shot."*

He shook his head.

"*Here.*" He held his sketch pad out. "*A peace offering. I figured I'd need one if you actually showed up.*"

I took the pad from him and pulled it over to look at what he had drawn. It was a night scene. Two black silhouettes in a creek as dark bird-like things swooped down towards the creek. The figures were holding hands, their faces pressed together in a kiss.

"*I hate you.*" I smiled.

"*So? Peace?*" He grinned widely.

I looked up at him. "*Peace.*"

"*Do you think the art class paid off?*" He pulled his knees to his chest.

"*You're even better than you were during last summer.*" I nodded as I stared down at the sketch. "*And you were fucking great then.*"

He smiled at me.

"*Thank you.*"

"*Are we just friends during summer?*" I asked.

"*Yeah,*" he said. "*Not during school. Keep yourself away from this catastrophe.*"

"*I meant...are we just friends during summer?*"

He was staring at me again.

"*Or...are we something else?*"

"*Like super best friends?*" He cocked an eyebrow. "*I can do super best friends.*"

"*You know what I mean,*" I said. "*Don't play games with me.*"

"*I don't really like games anyway.*" He nodded. "*We're the best of friends. Period.*"

"*Are you gay, Ian?*" I asked.

"*Yes.*"

"*I'm bisexual.*"

"*Figure that out finally?*" The corner of his mouth turned up.

"*I guess,*" I said. "*Well, I mean, at least for you. Haven't really found any other guys I wanted to...ya' know.*"

"*Sexuality is a tricky thing.*" He nodded. "*Especially when you're a teenager.*"

"*You seem pretty sure of yours.*"

"*I'm usually pretty confident about most things.*"

"*So...why not me?*" I couldn't look him in the eyes.

"*Because...because I care about you, Mike,*" he said. I knew he was looking me in the face. "*A lot.*"

I finally looked up at him.

"*I'm going to keep asking you for more.*" I gave him a firm look. "*All summer. Every summer.*"

"*I won't get mad.*"

"*Okay,*" I said. "*So, do you want to make out or rub up against each other like wild animals?*"

He laughed loudly.

"*You are completely incorrigible.*"

"*The worst you can say is 'no,' so I figured why not ask?*" I shrugged with a smile.

"*I'll think about it.*"

"*You owe me a kiss.*" I reminded him. "*You promised.*"

"*I promised you a kiss before the end.*" He held a finger up. "*And this is very obviously not the end.*"

I relented.

"*I will get that kiss.*"

"*I promised you.*" He nodded.

"*So...what are you going to show me this summer?*"

"*Not what you think.*" He frowned, disapprovingly.

"*That's not what I meant.*" I laughed loudly.

"*Wanna live off of the land?*" He asked. "*We can camp all summer.*"

"*I've never really camped.*" I chewed at my lip.

"Well, the trick is to set up camp within walking distance of a convenience store so that you have easy access to food." He nodded earnestly. *"But not too close. It's all about roughing it, after all."*

I brayed.

"Or we could just camp out tonight." He shrugged with a smile. *"Tell scary stories, go swimming...that kind of thing."*

"Then make out and dry hump."

He frowned at me.

"Okay, okay." I rolled my eyes. *"I'll give it a rest."*

He grinned.

"For now."

He rolled his eyes.

That night, right before dusk, we met deep in the woods. Ian showed me how to set up a tent since I'd never done it before. He showed me how to drive the stakes down at an angle to better secure the tent. He taught me how to build a fire the best way. Then he told me the scariest stories he knew—which were more funny than scary—but I think he knew that I was nervous to be camping anyway and took it easy on me. Then, just past midnight, he showed me an old field that had once been used for cattle grazing, where there was still a fairly large watering hole. It wasn't deep into summer yet, so it was full, and the water was pretty clean.

We stripped down to our boxers and swam until we were worn out. Afterward, we went back to our tent and climbed in, shivering and just dry enough from our swim. We crawled on top of our sleeping bags and pulled the covers over us that he had brought. When I inched up behind him and draped my arm over him, he let me. But he warned me to keep my hand in reasonable places—*"i.e., above the waist.*" And I did. But not an inch of his chest or stomach went unexplored by my fingertips.

All summer long, it was "The Ian and Mike Show" again. We camped numerous times; we went on hikes. He taught me about different bird species, introduced me to local lizards and snakes—helping me to determine which were poisonous and which weren't. We swam numerous times at midnight, but we didn't hold hands or kiss. If I asked, he reminded me that *"this isn't the end, Mike."* But he still let me look at him all I wanted. To gaze longingly, and quite often, lasciviously, at his body. When we hiked, he always stripped his shirt off. Most people would assume it was to stay cooler, but I knew it was for my benefit. I took advantage of those times, making sure to memorize every inch of his torso.

He never showed up for our excursions with a bruise or split lip. The summer seemed to be the best time of the year for Ian. His spirits were always lifted during the warmer months when the sun was around to provide the most light. I began to worship the summer again. Reveling in all of the extra light. It meant that I got to spend as much time with my friend as the summer holidays allowed. When summer drew to a close, and we were once again standing in the creek, watching the bats, my heart was in my stomach. Ian even let me hold his hand again.

It was our tradition, after all.

"I want the next nine months to hurry up," I whispered to him as the bats swooped down that night.

Ian just smiled at me and agreed. That night, when we left the creek and exited the woods, I watched him walk in the direction of his home for a few minutes, then trailed behind him. After several minutes of walking, barely keeping Ian's figure in my sights in the dark, I realized that he lived in an area of town that wasn't exactly the nicest...or safest. I swallowed my fear and followed at a distance, desperate to know about Ian away from school. When we reached one of the most run-down neighborhoods in town, Ian walked up into the yard of one of the only decent homes and approached the front door.

I dashed into a neighboring yard and hid behind a large tree, watching with morbid curiosity as he swung the door open. And the screaming began. I watched in fear at what transpired in the doorway, and then in horror as it spilled out onto the front lawn. The fight was very quick, and Ian didn't come out of it unscathed. When it was all said and done, my best friend was still standing, but his father wasn't. Then I watched as my best friend marched into the house and slammed the door behind himself. His father moaned and groaned on the front lawn for a really long time, rolling around like a wounded animal.

Finally, his father managed to get to his feet and stumbled drunkenly, in agony, toward the house. Apparently, Ian had locked the door behind himself. For several minutes, his father pounded on the door and screamed. He even tried kicking at the door, to no avail. Then he slumped down on the porch and fell asleep. Tears were trailing down my cheeks when I finally ran out of the neighbor's yard. I didn't stop running or crying until I was in my own safe home in my bed and asleep.

The following Monday, the first day of sophomore year, when Ian walked through the main hallway, all the other students sliding out of his way, he had two black eyes and a cut on his cheek. The evidence that what I had seen was not just a really bad dream. I started to wave at him, but his eyes flicked to me quickly, pleading with me. So, I turned back to my locker and pretended that I hadn't seen him. It broke my heart.

That day at lunch, I was sitting at my table, digging into my food, waiting on my "friends" when Kevin approached me. I looked up at him, my hamburger halfway to my mouth. *My buh-brother graduated luh-last year.* He explained, then lowered his tone to barely a whisper. *Ian said I shuh-should sit wuh-with you.* I glanced over at Ian. He was sitting across the cafeteria, by himself, looking out at nothing. I told Kevin that, of course, he could sit with me. The gratitude was evident as he slid into the seat across from me.

No sooner had he sat down than suddenly three large figures were behind him. I looked up, my burger almost to my mouth again, to find Carson, Jon, and Martin looming behind Kevin. I set my burger back down on my tray as my stomach knotted up. *Fag.* That's the only thing that Carson could think of to sneer down at Kevin. Kevin's face turned green as he looked over at me in fear. I looked up at Carson. "*Go bother somebody else, asswipe,*" I growled at him. Then his hands were on my shirt and he was starting to drag me across the table.

Then I was violently sliding back into my seat. I looked up to see Carson's head being slammed into the table. Then he was lifted up and a fist flew into his face. And Carson went down. Martin and Jon scattered. It all happened so quickly that I didn't have time to really register it immediately. Ian was standing there, glaring down at Carson on the ground. Carson wasn't moving or making a sound. Ian looked up, angrier than I had ever seen him. He turned, looking at everyone in the cafeteria.

Everything was frozen in time and deathly silent as everyone stared at him.

"This is the only warning I'm giving any of you fuckers," he said just loudly enough so that everyone would hear. *"Keep your fucking hands to yourselves."*

He glanced at me so quickly that I almost missed it. His mouth formed the word *"sorry."* Then he was walking calmly out of the cafeteria as Carson started to groan from the floor. Mrs. Boudreaux, one of the AP English teachers rushed over to check on Carson. *"Go to Principal Morton's office now, Ian!"* She screamed in that vacuum of silence. *"That's where I'm headed, Mrs. Boudreaux,"* Ian replied evenly without even turning his head.

He's so fucking cool, I thought as my stomach fluttered.

And sexy.

Carson getting his ass handed to him at lunch was all anyone would talk about for the rest of the day. And the weeks and months that followed. Ian had added to his reputation and legend at the school. When he was back in classes the very next day—not even one day of suspension, it only added to the legend. No one was any nicer to Ian, though. But Jon and Martin were not seen hanging out with Carson anymore. And Carson never touched another person as far as I knew. In fact, he barely said a word to anyone for the rest of his high school career. Since he was a senior the year Ian knocked him out in the cafeteria—and everyone else had been warned—the school became a fairly decent place for the rest of my high school years.

That event was when I truly fell in love with my best friend.

I knew that nothing would change that.

And the next nine months passed with Ian not talking to me and pretending he didn't see me. But Kevin sat with me every day—and right after Ian sat down at his table far away, I'd see him glance over to make sure that Kevin was sitting where he had told him to sit. If Ian defending Kevin and myself hadn't made me fall in love with him—those daily glances would have. I began counting down the school days, waiting for summer to come. Waiting for the light hours of the days to stretch out longer and longer.

Chapter 6

Mike
Sophomore Spring Break

Before I even snuck out of my window, I was mad at myself. I had promised my best friend that I would leave him alone during the school year. Not get involved in his life so that I would be safe from the barbs that he had thrown his way every single day. But I hadn't spent time with him in more than half a year, and I felt like I was coming out of my skin. Like I was withdrawing from some illicit substance. I had paced my room for hours that night before I finally settled into my decision and crept out of my bedroom window.

Once again, I found myself dashing through my neighborhood at night and through town under the cover of darkness, on my way toward the woods. When I was safely ensconced in the woods, I pulled my pack of cigarettes out of my pocket and put one in my mouth. Nervously, I lit one as I stood just beyond the tree line. What if Ian got pissed that I intruded on his late-night swims? Would he even be swimming? It wasn't really all that warm yet. The water might be too cold.

I smoked like a freight train as I made my way through the dark of the woods, wondering if I was making the worst decision for our friendship. Would I piss Ian off if I just came to the creek to watch him for a while? To just rememorize the curves and angles of his body again? To just look him in the eyes from a distance and give him a smile? Get one in return? I wouldn't force him to talk to me or anything—just look me in the eyes. Maybe wave.

When I saw the creek ahead, bathed in blue moonlight, I smiled and stomped out my cigarette, my pace increasing. I heard splashing in the distance and my smile grew even wider and I found myself jogging towards the creek. But before I got to the creek, I stopped myself. If I burst through the trees and ran to the bank of the creek and found my friend, he'd know how desperate I had been to see him. That that had been my plan when I walked out there that night. So, I lit another cigarette, took a deep breath, and then strolled casually towards the creek.

Keeping a smile off of my face, I approached the creek bank, trying to look as casual as possible. I looked down in the creek, expecting to see my friend. And I did. But he wasn't alone. It took a couple of moments for everything to register in my brain. I turned quickly and walked back into the woods. But I didn't go far. I sunk down behind a tree and stared out at the night. I smoked cigarette after cigarette, occasional splashing coming from the creek behind me. Then everything was quiet.

Minutes...maybe hours...later, I heard someone moving through the woods. I glanced over to see the dark shape move through the woods, walking back toward town. But it was just the one figure. And it wasn't Ian. When I was sure that the guy was gone, I slowly rose from my spot at the base of the tree and headed back toward the creek. When I approached the bank, I looked down into the creek again. There was only one figure in the creek now.

Ian was standing in the water, completely naked, the water providing a little modesty as he stared up at the sky.

"I can see the glow of your cigarette," he said softly.

I didn't answer.

"Are you coming in?" He asked after a beat.

I didn't get in. I stomped out my cigarette and made my way back through the woods. When I got home, I wasn't angry. I was aroused and curious, and...*jealous*. I didn't try to see my friend again for the rest of the school year. I had learned my lesson.

Chapter 7

Mike
Summer Before Junior Year

Sophomore year ended. And I went to find Ian. I didn't hesitate this time. I didn't worry about whether or not he wanted me to find him. The long days of summer were beginning—and this was what we did. Summer was our agreement. The season with the most light, we were allowed to be friends. So, I didn't pretend that I didn't know where I'd find him. I made my way past the creek to the trail where I had first seen him throw a punch. A punch that left a psychological and emotional scar for him.

Ian was sitting at his tree again. His sketchpad was against his knees and he was peacefully sketching. Just like always. The cut over his eyebrow was still angry and raw-looking. The cut he came to school with a few days before school ended. I went directly to him and sat down, just like I always did, and waited for him to finish his sketch. The charcoal scratched across the paper for a few minutes, then he finally looked up. His expression was blank as those iceberg eyes stared out from their milky pools.

"*I didn't watch,*" I said.

"*I know.*"

"*What was that about?*" I asked. "*Is it love?*"

He just looked at me.

"*Or was it just lust?*"

"*It was neither,*" he replied.

"*Then what was it?*" I demanded.

"*Solace.*"

We stared at each other for a very long time. And just as Ian had taught me over two previous summers, I held his gaze. I didn't lose my resolve. I didn't back down.

"*Who are you even?*" I tried to control myself, but it came out as a whimper.

"*What do you mean?*"

"*Why do you go out of your way to hurt me?*"

"*How did I set out to hurt you, Mike?*"

"*Don't play games. We only play one game—and this isn't it.*" I spat. "*You know that I saw what happened, so don't play dumb.*"

"*I do know that you saw it.*" He nodded, calm and collected. "*But I didn't invite you into the woods. We had agreed that we wouldn't meet up during the school year. You gave me your word on that. I had no way of knowing that you'd wander out into the woods to find me. So, what you saw...that's your fault. Not mine. I didn't set you up to be hurt, Mike. If you had stuck to our agreement, you'd be none the wiser.*"

"*You know that I'm...that I'm...*"

"*You're in love with me?*"

"*Yes!*" It came out so angrily that I scared myself. He nodded. "*I do know that.*"

"*Then why?*" I reached out and grabbed him by the collar of his shirt.

It was the dumbest thing I'd ever done. If Ian had wanted, he could have laid me out with one punch. Blackened an eye. Knocked out a tooth. Wailed on me until I was left broken and bleeding on the trail. His expression didn't change as I shook him by his collar and screamed in his face, my eyes never leaving his. After I started to wear myself out, he raised his hands and gently pried my fingers away from his collar. He barely had to put forth any effort. I had torn his shirt. His eyebrow cut was seeping blood. He held my hands for a moment, then he pulled off his tattered shirt, wadded it up, and pressed it to the cut to staunch the flow of blood, his expression not changing, though I knew it had to hurt.

"*Because you are more than solace to me,*" he said finally, staring back. "*You aren't just comfort or one single need. You're all of them. That's why.*"

"*Why can't I be...that...too?*" I was crying.

Ian used his hand that wasn't holding his shirt to his head and ran a thumb under each of my eyes, wiping away tears as they came. He pulled the bloodied shirt away from his head. The cut was no longer bleeding. I sat there crying as he stood up and dropped the destroyed t-shirt at his feet. He kicked off his flip-flops and his hands went to the button of his shorts. He unbuttoned and unzipped his pants. Then he shoved them to his ankles and stepped out of them. Next, he slid his boxers off.

Ian stood there, naked, in broad daylight next to the tree just off the trail, I stood up quickly, in complete shock. His torso and legs were littered with bruises of varying shades. I didn't even want to see his back.

"*If you think that will fix...this...then fine.*" He shrugged and held his arms out. "*Give me solace, Mike. Fix me.*"

The last two words were like a hammer to my gut. I went to Ian, but I didn't touch him in the way that he said I could. I wrapped my arms around him and pulled him into me. I hugged him. Ian's face was in my neck, and he made no noise, but I felt his tears burning a hot trail down my neck and pool near my collarbone. Ian was so broken. And I wasn't helping.

An hour later, I had made a trip back to my house and returned with a fresh t-shirt for Ian. I was cleaning the cut over his eyebrow with peroxide and cotton balls as he sat in front of me, no longer nude. He didn't wince or grimace, he just sat there, his hands in his lap as I cleaned the wound. The peroxide was bubbling like crazy, so I knew it had to hurt. He didn't show it on his face. But his hands clenched every now and then.

"*Is your dad in the Gulf now?*" I asked.

"*Yes.*"

"*Why do you let him do this to you?*" I wasn't asking Ian; I was asking the wind.

But Ian was the one who answered.

"*I don't like hitting people who aren't my father,*" he said. "*It's even harder to hit him.*"

"*Someone who fights like you?*" I asked. "*It's hard to believe that. But I do.*"

"*Thank you.*" He closed his eyes as I patted at the wound.

"*But I really meant—he wouldn't be able to lay a hand on you if you didn't allow it,*" I whispered. "*He wouldn't have the chance. So, why do you let him land any?*"

"*It's better me than my mom,*" he replied. "*If he wears himself out on me, then I put an end to it, he's too tired to fight anymore.*"

It made sense, but in the worst way.

"*I'll fucking kill him.*"

It was the first time I had said something like that. And the weight of how much I truly meant it scared me.

"*Don't. Not right now.*" A single tear slid down Ian's cheek.

"*I don't want him to hit you anymore,*" I said firmly.

Ian looked up at me. I stared back, pushing that message into him with the fierceness in my eyes.

"*Okay,*" he said.

"*If he hits you again, I won't be your friend anymore,*" I mumbled.

"*He won't hit me anymore.*" Ian agreed, his eyes sliding closed again.

Ian knew what I meant. He wasn't to allow his father to bruise or batter him anymore. He could knock his dad out all he needed to, but if he held back and let his dad break him again, our friendship was over. That's how much I loved Ian.

"*And if you need solace…just don't need solace,*" I said.

"*Will you hug me when I need comfort?*" He whispered.

His voice came out sounding like he was his actual age for once.

"*Yes.*" I exhaled. "*Anytime. Any place.*"

"*Okay.*" He opened his eyes as I pulled the cotton ball away from his brow. "*I'm sorry, Mike.*"

"*I'm sorry, too, Ian,*" I replied.

Then I put triple antibiotic on his cut and covered it with a bandage. Ian fell into me, wearing my favorite t-shirt, and wrapped his arms around me. I wrapped my arms around him and held him against me. It was way past dark before we let go of each other and went our separate ways to our own houses. That night, I slept soundly, confident that when Ian's dad came back from the gulf at the end of summer, he would be in for a shock. His son, my best friend, had made me a direct promise. Ian would not allow himself to be hit anymore by his father.

For the first part of summer, Ian and I camped more, swam more, and he taught me even more. His well of knowledge about *everything* seemed bottomless. At night, we'd lay under the stars in grassy fields, and he'd point out constellations and explained how navigation can be done by the stars. During those nights, he'd let me hold his hands, run my fingers along his palm, lace my fingers between his. On hot days he introduced me to the sweet nectar of honeysuckle. Once, when some honeysuckle nectar dribbled onto my chin, without thinking, he licked it off of my chin with a laugh. When he realized what he had done, he blushed, then immediately changed the subject to something else. One night he showed me how to hitch a ride to the next town over so that we could sneak into one of the only few drive-ins left in the area.

Then we walked miles to the lake, and he showed me how to fish. He taught me which fish were good to eat, which ones were too small and had to be tossed back to the lake. How to scale and clean a fish. How to roast it over an open fire. How to bait a hook even. All of these things I'd never been taught. He took me with him when he changed the oil in an older neighbor's car for her and showed me how to do that. How to change a flat tire. He taught me more about being a man than my own father had.

And he was always willing to sketch anything that I asked him to sketch. One day, as we were sitting by the creek on a Sunday morning, when it was free of other kids, he was sketching a bird for me. That's when I broached a topic I had not yet been brave enough to bring up.

"What's it like?" I blushed.

"Drawing?" He didn't look up.

"Having sex?"

A nervous laugh escaped my throat. He didn't laugh at me or tease me.

"I think it's different for everyone," he answered earnestly. *"Like masturbation...but warmer, more sensual, more exhilarating. Intimate. Uncomfortable. Awkward. Explosive. Joyful. Gross. Arousing. It's everything wrapped into one."*

I sat there and watched him draw a little while longer.

"You've had a blowjob, right?"

"Mmm," he answered simply.

"Have you...given one?"

"Mmm."

"What's it like?"

"Do you want to find out?" He asked, looking up from his sketchpad.

"Hell yes." I laughed loudly.

I made to move toward him.

He held a hand out and stopped me with a laugh. His charcoal black fingers smudged my t-shirt. I didn't care.

"I didn't mean that."

"Tease."

"I can get you a blowjob." He grinned. *"You're bisexual still, right?"*

"Yes..."

"Okay." He nodded. *"Let's meet at the creek tomorrow. Noon."*

"What?"

"Do you want to find out what a blowjob is like?" He cocked an eyebrow.

"Well...I...think so...yes." I was confused.

"Creek. Tomorrow. Noon."

That whole night, trying to sleep was impossible. I stayed aroused off and on throughout the night, wondering what my friend had in store for me at noon the next day. I was turning seventeen in a few days— I knew about sex and girls and boys and all of that stuff. And I wanted to experience it all. But it made sleep nearly impossible when I thought about what Ian might do to me the next day. The most arousing thoughts I'd ever had flashed through my head all night. Even when I did manage to sleep, my dreams were X-rated.

The next day, I made my way to the creek, just as Ian had instructed me, at noon. When I got to the creek, it took me a moment to spot Ian, but he was standing next to his tree, talking to some girl that I knew was a grade ahead of us at our high school. When I came out of the tree line and approached the bank of the creek, Ian spotted me, then pointed and said something to the girl. She looked over at me, kind of shrugged her shoulders, then waved me over. I wanted to be offended by the *"yeah, I guess so"* gesture...but I was too enthralled and excited.

Ian gave me a wink and sat down by his tree and started sketching as the girl took my hand and led me into the woods. And a hundred yards away from screaming and swimming teenagers, I had my first blowjob. It didn't last long. But it was exciting and scary and uncomfortable and embarrassing and the best feeling I'd ever had in my life. When the girl and I parted ways, I admitted that it was one of the best things ever, no matter how embarrassed I was. However, it wasn't everything, as Ian had said. Because it was with the girl—whose name was Catherine, which I didn't find out until days later. I had wanted it to be with Ian—so it wasn't the best thing ever. It wasn't everything.

When I got back to the tree, Ian was still sitting there, sketching a figure jumping into the creek. He looked up at me, his hand pausing on the paper, charcoal pinched between his fingers. He cocked an eyebrow at me, I gave him a nod, and he smiled. Then he went back to his sketch. I sat down across from him and watched him sketch. And we never spoke of it again.

I met that girl several more times throughout the summer, but not just for blowjobs. I got to touch boobs for the first time, learned how to finger and perform oral sex on a girl, learn how to put a condom on at the girl's instruction, have actual sex for the first time—and yeah, there were plenty of other blowjobs. But...most of all, I finally understood solace. After a while, I began to wonder if Ian had set things up so that I could learn about sex...or solace. Either way, he had found another way to teach me, without even being present.

No matter the lesson, halfway through summer, I had decided on one thing. I wouldn't have sex again. Until it was with Ian. And I knew that I would wait as long as it took. Sex was great...but the main lesson I learned was that it had to be even better with a person that I cared about. A person I loved. So, my sights homed in on the person I knew I loved more than any other. Who I would love more than anyone else in my entire life. Ian.

Ian Chambers.

I was seventeen years old at the end of summer and his name was still my mantra. The mere thought of his name could arouse me. Not actually give me an erection or anything—that would have been crazy— but it did something to the innermost parts of me. It made me tingle. Warm. His name, when it went through my head late at night as I was waiting for sleep to overtake me, made me close my eyes and smile in rhapsody.

Ian Chambers.

It was almost too much for my teenage mind and body to handle. I found myself wondering if he knew the effect he had over not just my body but my mind.

Ian.

Ian.
Ian.

Waves of pleasure flowed through my body, that no orgasm would ever match, when I merely thought of his name late at night. My belly fluttered and ached when I thought about how many hours I'd have to wait to see him again. The last time that I had sex with that girl, I did it angrily, bitterly. It wasn't sex. It wasn't solace. It was frustration being released. It was anger and frustration with Ian. He was denying me the one thing that would make me feel like a complete person. Even when I finally released at the end of my thrusting into her, I wanted more. But not from her. She would never be enough. She was a nice enough girl. Sexually liberated and open. Always kind to me. Never said or did anything to intentionally make me feel awkward. But she wasn't Ian. And she never would be.

I'd find myself wracking my brain, wondering why Ian was denying me. Was he taunting and teasing me? Was he playing a game with me? He'd let me stare at his body, he'd shown himself to me naked, he let me touch him in ways that no other boy had. But there were limits to that generosity. Always boundaries. He'd let things go just this side of too far, then retreat. Why would someone do that to another person? Either give yourself over completely or not at all!

Then, one night, it struck me like a punch to the chest as I waited for sleep to overtake me in my bed. Ian was giving me what he was mentally and emotionally capable of giving me. When he pushed back, I hadn't reached his boundaries. I had long gone past them. He was doing everything he could to give me as much of himself as he could. He wasn't trying to be cruel—even if he inadvertently was—he was trying to make me happy. That frustrated me more than anything. The anger rose within me and made me fume.

The next day, when I met Ian in the woods, he was sitting by his tree off of the trail. *I want you to teach me to fight.* I had commanded angrily, kicking dirt at him. Ian pursed his lips and blew over his sketchpad, blowing away dirt. He sketched for a few more moments, then looked up at me, his hand still against the sketchpad. *Frustrated and angry?* He asked, his head cocked to the side. *Hell yes, I am, you fucking asshole.* He nodded. *Punch that tree right there. Hard as you can.* He flicked his head toward a tree with a thick trunk, covered in jagged bark, a yard away from me.

What? I seethed down at him. *If you punch that tree as hard as you can, I'll teach you to fight if you want.* Without thinking, I spun towards the tree. I threw my fist out with all of my might. My knuckles connected with the tree trunk. Immediately, overwhelming pain shot through my fingers, throughout my hand, and up my forearm, settling in my bicep. *Fuck!* I screamed. *I broke my fucking hand! Fuck! Fuck!*

Ian set his sketchpad down calmly and stood. I was dancing around, shaking my fist, tears welling up in my eyes. Ian took my hand in his and looked at it. *It's not broken, Mike.* He spoke. I stopped flailing around, but I was still shifting from foot to foot as he held my hand. I was aroused. And Ian would have had to have been blind to not notice. Ian looked up at me, then bent his head down and kissed my knuckles. They were shredded and starting to seep blood. He didn't care. *Do you think you hurt the tree?*

I frowned at him, confused. *Did it learn a lesson?* He cocked an eyebrow at me.

I just stared at him. *Or do you think that, maybe, if it was a person, it would just be humiliated? What do you think trees feel? Do you think they can feel degraded?* I felt my anger going away. *Do you think anything that is attacked really understands what is happening? Do you think you'd feel better if the tree felt like your hand and you were fine? Do you want to make people physically feel how you feel inside?*

I looked down.

Ian turned my hand over and opened it. I hissed. He bent down and kissed the palm of my hand gently.

I don't want to learn to fight anymore, I whispered.

I know. He nodded before kissing each of my fingertips. Then his lips were on my wrist. The inside of my forearm. The inner curve of my elbow. I was so aroused. He kissed my bicep. His fingers found the hem of my shirt and raised it. His lips found my collar bone. My left pec. Then my right. The middle of my chest. He bent and his lips found my stomach. And my whole body jerked as I released in my shorts.

Ian pulled me into a hug as my body spasmed over and over, but he held on tightly, letting me jerk and twist in his arms. It seemed to go on forever. I had never orgasmed so hard or for so long when I had had sex with Catherine. When I finally stopped spasming, and my cheeks were in full blush, Ian raised his head to my ear and whispered. *Showing kindness is a lot better way to deal with frustration and anger than hitting something. Nobody—nothing— should have to feel the way you feel right now.*

He didn't tease me for blowing a load in my pants from merely having him kiss me. He hadn't even touched me in a way that was overtly sexual—but he brought me to orgasm in seconds with a few simple kisses. Not the kiss he had promised me—these kisses were something else.

I don't feel that way anymore. I had said.

I don't want you to ever feel that way. He whispered in my ear again. *I'm sorry if Catherine just frustrated you. That wasn't what I intended.*

She isn't you. I whispered back.

His lips kissed the lobe of my ear. I didn't orgasm again, but my body involuntarily jerked.

I love you. I sighed.

I believe you. He replied and hugged me tighter.

The last few weeks of summer, I didn't go into the woods with Catherine anymore. I had made a promise to myself. Pledged my fidelity to one person. And I stuck by it. Ian and I did more fishing, more stargazing, more camping, more sketching, a lot more laughing. And anytime I felt angry or frustrated, he kissed his way up my arm and over my chest and down my stomach. The result was always the same. But I was never allowed to touch him like that. To bury my face in his chest and stomach, to inhale his scent, to feel his skin under my lips.

At the end of summer, we stood in the creek at midnight and watched the bats hunting for their dinner again. We held hands again. My knuckles were mostly healed. Ian let me hug him when the bats were done searching out food and his hands rested in the valley of my back. *Lower.* I had whispered. He acquiesced, trailing his fingers down the light blonde hairs in the valley of my lower back. And then his hands settled on my ass under the water. It was the best ten seconds of my life.

Then it was time to go our separate ways. But, of course, I trailed Ian home, watching him as he cut his way through the dark of his bad neighborhood. He knew I was there, somewhere behind him. And I knew that he knew. I hid behind the same tree as he walked up into his yard. He had barely set foot on his property when the front door of his house swung open violently. His dad charged from the inside of the house, down the porch steps, and right at Ian. I cringed.

Ian's father was on the ground before I even saw it happen. And he wasn't moving. Ian's head raised ever so slightly as he stood there. *I don't break my promises to you, Mike.* He said it just loudly enough that I could make it out. His voice had a quiver to it. Then he went into his house and closed the door. I knew, without being able to hear it, that he had latched and locked the door tightly. I waited around just long enough to make sure that his father moved and wasn't dead. But it was more to make sure that Ian wouldn't be in trouble. It was the only reason that I cared if his father was alive or not.

The following Monday, it was the first time that I saw Ian walk down the main hall of the high school, not a single bruise in sight. When he passed me, he gave the smallest of nods and something akin to a smile. It made the remaining nine months of the school year somewhat tolerable.

I didn't try to find Ian after school or during school holidays or breaks. But we met halfway. Kind of. Sometimes, I'd look over Kevin's shoulder at lunch, to Ian sitting by himself across the cafeteria. He'd look over at me for a few seconds, wiggle his eyebrows, then go back to his food. Sometimes, he'd stand from his table and reach upwards to stretch, exposing a sliver of his stomach. Then he'd look over at me blandly before going back to his food. A few times, when we passed in the hallway, his fingers would brush against mine. It wasn't much—but it was so erotic.

I found myself wishing that the lightest days of the year would arrive.

Chapter 8

Ian

"Are you cold?" Mike asked as we sat there by the creek.

"A little," I said as I pulled my t-shirt back on.

Mike wrapped his arms around me and pulled me into him. It wasn't really cold. The breeze was warm early in summer and the water had still been fairly warm from having the sun beat down on it all day long. But it wasn't my body that felt chilled. It was everything else. The last four years. Everything had brought this chill on—the loss of all of my warmth. And...I wanted Mike to hold me if I was being totally honest with myself.

My warmth would return.

In time.

I just had to be more patient than it.

"*I love you,*" Mike whispered against my ear.

His breath was soft and warm against my ear.

"I love you, too," I said softly.

Mike pulled back and stared at me, his arms still draped around me.

"You heard me," I stated evenly.

"How long have you loved me?" Mike asked, his voice low.

I turned my face to his.

"Since you were worried about the squirrel being dead," I replied. "Since I saw your heart."

Mike's eyes closed, but the tears still seeped out and rolled down his cheeks as he held me.

"When you asked me to be your friend," I said. "And you were such a geek in a god's body...I knew I loved you. Then, when I asked if you were gay and let you stare at me as I laid in the grass, I knew I loved you. When you stood there and watched the bats with me and grabbed my hand, I knew I loved you. When you bandaged my cut. When you punched the tree.

The wisteria. The real question is when *didn't* I know I loved you?"

"When didn't you know?" He asked.

"When I didn't know you existed," I said. "Once I knew you existed, well, there wasn't a time I didn't love you."

Mike was fully crying now as he held me.

"Couldn't you have just...once...forgotten about what being friends would have done to my reputation?" Mike breathed into my ear. "I've wanted you for so long."

"I'm sorry," I said.

It was all I could say.

Nothing would take it back.

Nothing changes the past.

I knew that my choice to distance myself from Mike at school had been wrong.

But how do you fix that?

"I forgive you." Mike sighed, his tears coming to a stop.

"And when you are annoyingly able to see my heart, under all of this, I love you even more," I said.

"Can I please...*touch you*?" Mike placed his hand against my cheek and turned my face to look me in the eyes.

I stared at him for several moments.

"Yes." I breathed out.

Mike's hands started to move.

"But, first, I want you to see something." I stopped him. "Please? You can touch me all you want afterward."

"Okay."

Mike didn't ask me if that was a promise. Because I hadn't broken a promise to him yet. Now that I had given him a kiss, he knew that everything I had ever promised had been done. It was almost midnight. It was the perfect time for what I wanted him to see.

"Come on." I stood and held my hand out to him.

Mike used my hand to hoist himself up. I stripped my shirt off again and led us back out of the tree line and down the bank of the creek again. We shimmied down into the water and I led him to the middle. Now we could see the sky clearly between the two sides. I led him right to the middle of the creek, holding both of his hands. He smiled down at our hands as the water rippled around us.

"Look up," I said.

Mike's head tilted back. And his eyes grew wide. They actually looked green in this light.

"It's called the Full Strawberry Moon," I said before tilting my head back to look up at the moon with him. "The Algonquins named it that to signal it as the time to gather ripe, wild strawberries. It's also known as the Honey Moon, Mead Moon, and the Full Rose Moon. But...I like Full Strawberry Moon. It makes me think of summer. I got to spend time with you in summer. So, that's my favorite. It's also a blue moon tonight. A blue moon is the second full moon within a single calendar month. It only happens once or twice a year. Hence the *once in a blue moon* saying. People say that blue moons look bigger...some people even claim they look blue, and that's where they got the name. But the moon is always greyish or white— only atmospheric conditions on Earth or an eclipse can make it look different colors. The moon is constant, unyielding. At least...for our lifetimes."

I stared up at the moon as I held Mike's hands underneath the water's surface.

"It's so bright." Mike breathed out. "It's almost as good at spotlighting you as the summer sun is."

I tilted my head down to look at him.

"But I can see you perfectly no matter how much or how little light there is, Ian," he said. "You were never your brother. Or your father. Or even your mother. You were the best kid in school. *I see you, Ian. I've always been able to see you.* You emit your own light."

I pulled on Mike's hands, drawing him into me. As his body crashed into mine, I pressed my lips against his. His hands went to my face as mine went to his back. And, for once, without being prompted, they slid down to his ass.

Chapter 9

Mike
Summer Before Senior Year

When I got to the tree just off of the trail—*our tree*—Ian wasn't sitting there with his sketch pad. His sketchpad was there, but it was laid haphazardly next to the trunk. The pages were fanned out. Panic immediately settled in my chest and I began spinning around, looking for him. Had I missed him at the creek? Was he in the field where the hay would be gathered? Had he stopped at the store? He was always waiting at the tree off of the trail on the last day of school so that our summer could begin. The sun was high in the sky, beating down as I spun in panic, looking for my best friend.

"Up here, silly."

I jumped when his voice came from above me.

I looked up to find Ian sitting on the branch of a tree. He was pushing a wad of paper against the trunk of the tree, focusing intently on whatever it was he was doing. Suddenly, he pulled the wad of paper away from the tree, smiled at the tree, then dropped the paper the fifteen feet to the ground. He started to shimmy down, as deft at climbing a tree as a monkey. Finally, he jumped the last six feet to the ground and landed beside me. He looked up at the tree, smiling.

"Um, what are you doing?" I laughed nervously.

"I was sketching, and a woodpecker chick fell out of its roost," he said. *"I used a blank sheet of paper to pick him up and take him back up. I wanted to keep as much of my scent off of him as much as possible, so his mom doesn't reject him. Though, I think that whole 'birds and human scents' thing is a myth. I think he'll be okay."*

I stared at my friend as he stared up at the tree, smiling widely.

"Can I kiss you?" I asked without meaning to.

His head tilted down to look at me.

"*No.*" He cocked an eyebrow.

"*Okay.*"

"*Are you going to ask again later?*"

"*Yes.*" I nodded.

"*Okay.*"

"*I love you,*" I said.

"*I still believe you.*" He smiled widely.

"*You are insufferable.*" I laughed loudly. "*You are so utterly frustrating and annoying and…and…*"

"*Arousing, isn't it?*" He glanced down.

I sat down quickly. Ian didn't tease me or smirk or even grin. He went over to the tree and sat down, scooping up his sketchpad in the process. He made a table out of his knees again and placed the pad against them. Charcoal in hand, he looked over at me.

"*What's the biggest question you ask yourself each day?*" He asked, his hand moving on the paper, but his eyes stayed on mine.

"*What?*"

"*Every day,*" he said again. "*Do you ask yourself a particular question that enriches your life in some way? Like 'what is the meaning of life' or 'is there a God'…something like that?*"

I swallowed hard, willing my erection away.

"*I guess I usually ask myself every day if I'm a good person,*" I replied.

He nodded.

"*What about you?*"

"*I always ask myself if I had a magic wand, what would I do with it?*" He said, his eyes moving down to his sketchpad. "*Would I do good, or would I do evil?*"

I waited.

"*Have you answered it?*"

"*Do you think you're a good person?*" He asked, not looking up.

"*No*," I said. "*But I try harder every day.*"

"*I think I would do good*," he said. "*But I might be a little selfish. I might materialize a new family for myself. Or a new home. Or a car. Or the college of my dreams. Or...*"

I waited.

"*Or...what?*" I urged him on.

"*Or I'd make myself a better person so that I wouldn't be so selfish.*" He whispered it, not looking up.

"*You're the best person I know.*" I breathed out.

"*I'm not nearly good enough to you.*" And he did look up. "*I'm sorry I'm not everything you want, Mike.*"

I frowned.

"*You could be,*" I whispered.

He nodded.

"*Maybe,*" he said. "*Yes. Eventually. But not as I am. I'm...a mess. You know that, right?*"

I just looked at him.

"*One more year, Mike,*" he said, his hand still moving. "*That's all I ask.*"

"*Just one more?*" I chewed at my cheek.

"*Yes.*"

I sat back, now that it was safe to do so, propping myself up with my hands, lounging before him.

"*Do you ever stare at me?*" I asked.

"*All the time.*"

"*I've never seen you do it.*" I smiled. "*Unless you're sketching me.*"

"*You are so blissfully unaware of everything going on around you.*" He smiled back. "*It's easy to stare at you.*"

"*Stare at me now,*" I said lowly. "*Set your sketchpad down. And look at me. Go over my entire body with your eyes. From the top of my head to the tips of my toes. Stare at me like I stare at you.*"

Ian slowly let his knees unbend until his legs were sticking straight out and then slid his sketchpad off of his lap. At first, he looked in my general direction, then his eyes went to the top of my head. Slowly, sensually, his eyes traveled downward, over my forehead, his eyes connecting with mine, then leaving to travel over my nose, over my lips, down my neck, to my chest, my abdomen, my crotch, my thighs, my knees, my shins, my feet. Then his eyes were back on mine.

"*Your erection is back,*" he stated simply.

"*I don't care if you don't,*" I replied.

"*It's not bothering me.*"

"*Do you want it to?*"

"*Now who's insufferable?*" He laughed loudly.

"*I want to touch you.*"

"*No,*" he replied, bending his knees up to prop his sketchpad against them again. "*That's not the game we play.*"

"*Please?*" I groaned.

Ian's iceberg eyes flicked up to me and then back down as he started chewing on his bottom lip and his hand flew across his sketchpad. That was good enough for me. I rose to my knees, unconcerned with anything going on in my pants, and scooted over to kneel beside him. Ian was tense, but his hand didn't stop moving on his sketchpad.

Carefully, cautiously, I reached out as Ian continued to sketch...whatever it was he was sketching. I didn't take my eyes away from him in order to look at his sketchpad. Very softly, my hand touched his shoulder, laying there for the most satisfying of seconds before it slid down, over his chest, across it, then to just below his chest. I reached out with my other hand and reached to his face. His sketching stopped, but he didn't look up or move away.

I traced my thumb over his lips as if trying to memorize their shape and feel through touch. Ian stared down at his frozen hand on the sketchpad, as my hands explored his lips and just below his chest. I moved closer to him, bringing my face to within inches of his chest, and inhaled. He smelled like the wild. Like the woods and fields we spent our summers in, the creek that we held hands in at the end of summer each year. He smelled like the sun. Warm and dangerous. I closed my eyes as I inhaled, holding back a shiver. I was so aroused. My hand started to move lower, toward his stomach.

"That's enough, now." His hand was around my wrist and his eyes were open.

His hand had smeared my wrist charcoal black.

"Okay." I looked up into his eyes, expecting anger.

It wasn't anger. It wasn't sadness. It was wild. Feral. Longing. Arousal.

"Let's stop now," he said, but there was no power behind it.

"Okay."

But he didn't let go of my wrist. *God, he was so strong. He could break my wrist if he wanted.* That, too, was arousing. I knelt there, my breath caught in my throat as I stared into his eyes and he stared back with an intensity that I'd never seen before. His Adam's Apple bobbed up and down as our eyes stayed locked. Finally, he spoke:

"I'm going to let go now. Okay?" He whispered. *"Then I want to walk away for a minute."*

"You'll come back?" I breathed.

"Yes. I promise."

Then, he let go and I moved back, my arousal evident as I knelt there. When Ian rose to his feet, leaving his pad in front of the tree, it was very obvious that I was not the only one who had enjoyed my hands on him. Ian stiffly walked down the trail and kept going until he was out of sight. I closed my eyes with a sigh and fell back on my ass.

I pulled my knees up and laid Ian's sketchpad against them, making sure it was closed first. He hadn't invited me to look, so I didn't. I sat against his tree, waiting like I said I would. Ian had promised he'd come back, so I was going to wait as long as it took. I didn't have a watch on me, so I wasn't sure how long it was before I saw Ian coming back down the path. It hadn't been too long, but at least fifteen minutes had passed.

"I want to show you something," he said, looking down into my eyes as he approached. *"If you want to see it."*

"Okay."

I got up and handed Ian his sketchpad. He tucked it under his arm and motioned for me to follow. We walked down the trail where he had disappeared. Several minutes went by as we walked side by side in silence. Every now and then, I'd sneak a glance over at him. He was glancing at me at the same time, every time. We'd smile and look away from each other. After a bit, Ian looked at me and held a finger to his lips. He led me to the very edge of the woods, his footsteps becoming light. I mimicked his movements the best that I could.

When we got to the tree line, he held an arm out, stopping me. He pulled back a branch that was in our way, just enough so that we could peek out. We were just on the edge of someone's property. There was a somewhat ratty yard that looked like some effort had been made at mowing it, but it was mostly dirt with ragged weeds and rocks decorating it. The house sitting on the property was little more than a shack. On the porch, in a wheelchair, sat a man who looked old and broken, a blanket over his legs, but he couldn't have been that old.

I frowned as I looked at the man and Ian held his finger to his lips. He made sure that I was going to be quiet, then looked at the man, too. We watched for the longest time. Finally, the front door of the shack opened, and Carson stepped out. I almost gasped, but Ian looked at me and put his finger to his lips again. We turned our heads back to the scene at the house.

"*Are you doing okay, dad?*"

The man didn't respond.

"*I'm going to make dinner,*" Carson said to his wheelchair-bound father.

He knelt down and repositioned the blanket over his father's legs. Then he stood and leaned down to hug him.

"*I'll be back in just a few minutes, okay?*"

The man grunted.

Carson smiled and went back into the house.

Ian and I stood there for a few more moments, then he looked over at me and motioned for me to follow him. I blinked a few times, then let him lead me away from what we had just seen. Ian kept his fingers to his lips and led me through the woods again, not saying anything until we were back at the tree where he was always sketching in the woods. He sat down at the tree again, propping his sketchpad upon his knees. But he didn't move to open the sketchpad. I looked down at him for a moment, then sat down as well, folding my legs in.

"*Carson's parents were in a car wreck five years ago,*" he said. "*His mom died and his father...that's what happened to his father. He's been taking care of his father and himself since he was fourteen. Sometimes his aunt comes to help. But he's mostly alone.*"

"*Seriously?*"

He nodded.

"*He's not going to college or moving or going out to lead his own life. And, regardless of what other kids might say, he's pretty smart. He'll stay here and take care of his dad until his dad, inevitably, dies an excruciating death of some secondary illness. Probably pneumonia. And Carson won't be sorry for having chosen to stay and take care of him until the end. Whether that's tomorrow or forty years from now. He'll still be here.*"

I stared at Ian.

"*Why didn't you show me before?*" I asked.

"*Because all Carson has is his pride,*" Ian said. "*And I wanted him to keep that while he was still in high school.*"

"*Who all knows this?*"

"*Probably just the teachers.*" He shrugged. "*School administration. Adults.*"

Suddenly, I had a revelation. Whenever Carson picked on other kids, Ian gave him a chance to walk away. To save his pride. The only time he hadn't given Carson a chance was when he had his hands on me. And even then, he had jumped Carson and sucker-punched him when he couldn't see it coming. To show everyone that Carson hadn't had a chance to defend himself. To make it look like Carson only lost a fight because he was jumped suddenly. And he never hit him any more than he had to.

"Carson is not a bad person," Ian said. *"He has more sorrow than one human body can hold. Carson is a good person. He's a good son. He just...fucks up sometimes. He's human."*

I stared at Ian.

"You really see people, don't you?" I asked.

"I see you, Mike."

"It's summer." I smiled. *"It's the best time to see me. Lots of light."*

Ian smiled back, but it was sad.

It wasn't sadness at the acknowledgment that we only really got to spend time together in summer. His sadness was for Carson. And that made me fall even more deeply in love with Ian.

"I started coming to the woods at night five years ago because..."

I waited. I didn't want to prompt Ian or make him have a reason to not tell me what he was going to tell me.

"Because I'd sneak into the store and steal food and stuff for Carson," Ian said. *"I'd leave the bags for him and his dad on his porch. I did this for a while until one night he caught me. And his pride was so hurt. And he was so scared that I'd tell everyone about his family. His house. He attacked me. So, I had to hit him. He's never been mad about the punch. He's been mad that I pitied him. He's been scared that I might say something to everyone. But over the years, I never said a word to a soul. And I stopped pitying him. I only take a few bags of groceries once a month now. Now*

he's mad at me for caring. For not telling. Because not telling, to him, is still pity. He hates me for not hating him."

"After I'd drop off the groceries, I'd go to the creek. Swim alone. Talk to God. Ask why this happened to him. Why a kid would have that hand dealt to them. God was pretty quiet most of the time. And then, other times, I'd float in the creek, and look up at the moon, and I'd think...'if I had a magic wand, I wouldn't use it for me.' And I could swear...I mean, really swear...that God heard me."

"Do you think that God heard me?" He turned his face to me, tears silently streaming down his cheeks.

"Yes," I answered without thinking.

"Good."

Ian and I spent the first part of the summer camping, running wild in the woods, laying on hay bales, walking trails, swimming at night. It turned out to be an unusually mild summer throughout. And we worshipped in that temperate season. He sketched furiously. He said he wouldn't have much more time for sketching. I didn't know why he thought that. At the time, I didn't understand. But I tried to ignore that comment and focus on spending my days reveling in my friendship with Ian. The friendship that I loved but wanted to be so much more. Ian taught me the most important thing that summer.

He taught me about joy.

And he only had to teach me once.

A few weeks before the end of summer, we had both turned eighteen, and before our annual late-night creek swim and bat-viewing, we met in the field at dawn. Ian had the widest grin on his face as I approached him at his spot beside the hay bale on the northern side of the field. Before I could reach him, he stood, giddy and practically dancing like a live wire. I'd seen him happy before—but I'd never seen him quite so happy.

I want to show you something. He had said to me. His sketchpad was stuck under his arm like always. I smiled and nodded my head. I would never not agree when he wanted to show me...anything. But he didn't motion for me to follow. Instead, he grabbed my hand, lacing his fingers through mine, and he pulled me after him. The grin that split my face was almost painful it was so wide. He didn't walk—he practically ran, pulling me after him. We ran from the field to the woods. When we reached the woods, he let go of my hand so that we could make our way easily through the trees. I didn't like letting go of his hand, but I knew that he wouldn't have let go if it wouldn't have made our journey more difficult.

We seemed to walk forever, completely in silence, Ian grinning like an idiot the whole time. Several times I thought to ask him what we were walking so far into the woods to see. Further than we'd ever ventured into the woods before. However, I trusted him more than anyone, so I just followed, watching him as we made our way to wherever it was that we were going. The woods became so dense that we were ducking through limbs, pushing through foliage, getting slapped and poked by numerous plants, trees, and shrubs. A few yards later, Ian pushed through a particularly dense bunch of limbs and disappeared from my sight. I frowned to myself and hurried ahead, pushing through the same bunch of limbs, and nearly ran into Ian.

Ian was standing still, his head tilted upwards, that silly grin still affixed to his face. *What?* I breathed out as I stopped just before running him over. *Look.* He nodded upwards. I looked up. There was purple and green everywhere. This area of the woods was so much darker than the rest of the woods. The purple and green vines were blocking out most of the light, taking all of it for themselves. Small squares and circles of light managed to peek through here and there, but for the most part, the sun no longer belonged to us. It belonged to...whatever we were looking at. I turned, looking all around. The vines were climbing over everything, nearly making a room of purple and green around us.

What is it? I had gasped. He replied: *It's wisteria. It blooms in mid to late spring for only a few weeks. I've never seen it in summer, let alone this late. I think because it's been so cool this summer, and it's so deep in the woods, it's still blooming.*

I looked over at my friend—*the love of my life*—and he was so full of joy I could feel it. *It's beautiful.* I had told him. Ian smiled back at me, finally taking his eyes away from the ceiling of purple and green, then he walked over to some of the wisteria growing around us and inhaled deeply. I followed his lead. The smell made me jerk my face away for a split second. It was somewhat acrid, but floral and sweet...it smelled like how spring felt. Fresh, clean, hopeful. I shoved my face back into the wisteria and inhaled as deeply as I could, a smile spreading across my face.

Ian's face was buried in the flowering vines as well, taking in the smell of a spring that had refused to be banished. Everything in that room of wisteria was intoxicating. It overtook my senses and sensibilities. Before I could stop myself, I was reaching out for Ian. My hands grabbed him by his upper arms and pulled him toward me. But this was

Ian. He easily slipped out of my grasp, laughing like an imp as he leapt away like a wood nymph—a movement in direct contrast to the brute force he could call up at will and control with horrifying accuracy. It was so frustrating. And arousing.

Don't get too carried away. He wiggled his eyebrows at me. *I want you. Now. Give me what I want. Please?* He bit at his bottom lip—and I wanted to tackle him. Even if to just hold him against me, fully clothed. He considered me for a minute, his smile slowly fading away. *I want to sketch something for you.* He bit his lower lip again, the smile returning marginally.

The wisteria? I asked. *No.* He shook his head playfully. *Do you promise to keep your hands to yourself?* I squinted at him, wanting to be angry, but it was utterly impossible. *If I have to. Yes.* He nodded at me. He bent at his knees and set his sketchpad down carefully on the ground. His eyes settled on mine, burning into mine, as he kicked off his shoes. Then he slid his socks off, one at a time, his eyes never leaving mine. Then he pulled his t-shirt off over his head. He let it fall to the ground by his shoes.

There was a lump in my throat...and other places. Ian continued to gaze into my eyes as his fingers went to the button of his shorts. With a flick, the button was undone. Next, his zipper came down. Then the shorts were at his ankles. Then his boxers were at his ankles, and he stepped out of them. And he stood before me, naked and supernal. And...*aroused.* I swallowed hard.

He practically glided over to me, unashamed and unafraid. *Keep your hands to yourself now.* He ordered in a sing-song voice as he approached. All I could manage was a nod. Then his hands brought my shirt up over my head and pulled it off of me. It, too, got tossed to the pile of clothes he had started. Then his fingers were at the button of my shorts. Then the zipper. I was so aroused it was painful. He slid my shorts down and then my boxers, and when I stepped out of them, I was naked, too. I kicked my shoes off to complete the shedding of my clothes.

Ian bent forward slightly and placed his lips gently against my collarbone. I sighed. Then my left pec. Then the right one. Then a little lower to my stomach. I moaned, but I had learned some control. Ian stood up straight and looked me in the eyes. We were touching...in lower places. He didn't make a move to step away. And he didn't seem to mind. I shivered. I wasn't the least bit cold.

Ian grabbed my hand and led me over to the pile of clothes. *This is it.* I thought. *We're going to have sex. Finally.* But Ian pushed me down gently until I was sitting on top of the clothes. Then he looked around and found a fairly clear spot on the ground. He grabbed his sketchpad and went to the spot he had decided upon and laid down. He laid on his stomach, having to position himself so that he didn't hurt his groin. He laid there, on his stomach, propping up his upper half with his elbows, and pulled his sketchpad to where it was beneath his face.

I want you to describe me, Mike. He had told me. *Describe my body, and I'm going to sketch what you tell me.*

Seriously? It wasn't mocking. I was wondering if I really had permission to describe everything I saw in his body and what I thought about it.

Yes. He breathed out, charcoal in his hand, frozen against the sketchpad, his eyes closed with a look of pleasure on his face. *Describe what you see. What you think of it. What thoughts it gives you.*

Okay.

I took a steadying breath as I sat there, fully aroused, staring at the naked form of my friend. When I breathed out, I felt that I could do this. So...I described to Ian his hair. The summer growth, the way it curled slightly at the side of his head as if trying to tickle his ear. The way his button nose looked slightly upturned in profile. The plump apples of his cheeks that went down to an angular jaw and plump lips. His furrowed eyebrows as he concentrated on sketching as I described him. How I wanted to press my lips against his because they were practically begging to be kissed. How I imagined his tongue would feel against mine when I parted his lips with mine. How his skin would feel against my nose as I fed at his mouth.

Then I described his long, graceful neck and its curve as he laid there over his sketchpad. His defined and powerful arms that ended with delicate, artist's fingers that held as much strength as they did agility. The angles of his shoulder blades, how they seemed to be trying to cut through the skin of his back, and how they flexed as his arm moved over his sketchpad. The curve of his back down to the upward curve of his ass. The barely-there blond hairs I could only see when sunlight peeked through the wisteria at certain times. His muscular thighs and hair-dusted calves. How I wanted to run my tongue up from his calf, up the back of his thigh, up over his ass, up and along the length of his back, between his shoulder blades, leading to the side of his neck and then to his lips.

The arches of his feet strained and flexed as his toes dug into the ground below as if every part of him was full of untapped energy and possibility. Ian's expression was languid and dreamy as he sketched and listened to me. So...I told him that, too. I told how I imagined that he was thinking of my mouth on him—all over him. How he probably imagined that felt and how aroused it made him just to think it. How he wanted me to take control of him, to prove to him that he wanted to give himself over to me. To make him feel as loved as he made me feel. I wanted his shoulder blades to dig into the earth as I pushed him downwards and tried to make our bodies one.

I told him that even the sky agreed because when the sun did manage to peek through the wisteria above, it always found him. Squares of golden light decorated his back, his ass, the side of his face, his forearm. Even the sun desired his body as much as I did. To know him in a way that was rhapsodic. To feel everything divine his body had to offer. And I knew— without any shred of tangible evidence—that my body becoming one with his *would be* divine.

This probably went on for hours, our erections fading, but the sexual tension just grew as I devoured Ian's body with my eyes. When Ian was done sketching, he reversed his actions, redressing himself, and then me. It was nearly as erotic as being undressed by him. Then he picked up his sketchpad and tore out the sketch, handing it over to me. He had drawn himself perfectly, but also somehow managed to sketch himself the way that I saw him. Probably because I saw him for exactly who and what he was.

Ian and I walked out of the woods and once we were out of the woods, he held my hand as we walked through the field. The sun was setting, and the day had flown by. We had spent the whole day naked in the wisteria deep in the woods. And we had done nothing. And it was the best summer day I'd ever had. I asked to kiss him when we separated for the night, but he told me: "no." Somehow, I wasn't as upset by his answer as I usually was. Though, it was even harder to get him out of my head as I waited for sleep that night. His naked body kept jolting me awake just as I'd start to drift off. But it wasn't irritating or annoying or frustrating. It made me smile.

At the end of summer, we observed our annual ritual of watching the bats as we held hands, waist-high in the creek. When I asked Ian if I could kiss him after the bats were done feeding, he almost agreed. It took him several moments to answer. It topped all of the other enthralling moments I'd shared with him up until then. The anticipation, yearning, unfulfilled desire—it was absolutely intoxicating. The buildup over the years was more erotic than anything I'd done in the woods with Catherine the summer before.

But the same answer came out of his mouth at last. Not in the same way, though.

"*No.*" He leaned up to whisper in my ear, his lips against my ear, his jaw moving against my cheek. "*One more school year. Wait. Wait until I can give myself to you. Completely.*"

The thought made me shiver with delight.

Then his lips found the side of my neck.

And I really shivered.

He kissed me once. And I controlled myself. I didn't grab him or throw myself on him. I just moaned. Then he moved to the other side of my neck and kissed me there. Then the front of my throat.

"*I'm still...broken.*" His lips moved against my ear again. "*I'll put myself back together. For you.*"

"Put yourself back together for you," I whispered back, breathing in the scent of his hair that lay against my face.

Another kiss met my neck and then he was running away, towards his home. I watched him and smiled until he was completely out of sight. Then I turned and started to walk in the opposite direction, smiling like a lovesick teenager. Because I was. I had barely walked ten feet before something struck me in the gut. I turned my head to look off in the direction that Ian had run, and panic gripped me. I turned and ran as fast and hard as I could, trying to calculate how much of a head start I had given him.

I heard Ian scream for his father as I dashed behind the neighbor's tree by Ian's house and then the door of Ian's house flew open, and his dad came marching down the steps. Ian was standing in the middle of his lawn. Calm. Controlled. I couldn't see his face, but I didn't want to. I never wanted to see that side of Ian. His dad wasn't running or screaming, but he exuded anger. He was very obviously drunk and ready to murder.

Ian's mother was slumped against the door frame. I glanced at her quickly enough to notice the bruises and bloody face. Ian stayed still, waiting for his father to come to him. His father stepped up to Ian, his fist leading. It didn't even come close. That was how quick Ian was. Then another fist. Another easy dodge. Then again. And again. And again. Ian performed this dance with his father, barely having to work to avoid his father's fists, until his father was breathing heavily and barely able to stand straight.

Then Ian punched once. His father was lifted off of his feet and stumbled backward like a rag doll. Ian waited patiently as his father lay on the ground. Ian didn't make a move to go to his mother or stomp inside and lock the door. He waited. His father came to all fours, cursing and spitting, calling Ian names that I would never repeat as long as I lived. No one should ever be called those names. Ian moved over to his father so quickly it was almost supernatural, and his leg connected with his father's side, slamming into his ribs, sending him rolling. Ian went back to waiting.

It took his father longer to get to all fours again. Ian waited. Then his father somehow staggered to his feet. More curses and insults and proclamations about how he would kill Ian. Then he charged. Again, he was sent to the ground with a single hit. Ian didn't wait this time. His foot connected with his father's face this time. Even in the dark, I could see the almost black blood fly from his father's face as he went reeling from the kick. My fingers were digging into the tree. Ian's face was impassive. Blank. Unfeeling in this horrific moment.

His father lay on the ground, right beside the overgrown driveway, sputtering and coughing. Ian walked over to his father, bent down, and grabbed his father's arm. For a moment, I was worried that he'd help his father into the house. Instead, he just pulled him so that he was laying on his side. His father hacked up dark fluid. Puke and blood and then bile. Ian stood far enough back to avoid getting sprayed. When his father finally stopped puking and resorted to groaning and holding his side as he laid there, Ian went over and pulled his father's keys out of his pocket. He stepped back, pulled a key—I assumed, the house key—off of the keyring, then tossed the rest at his father. Ian finally spoke.

"Leave."

One word.

"*Fuck you!*" His father spat. "*Faggot!*"

Ian stood there for a few moments. Then he swung his leg back angrily. His father held his hands up defensively in fear. Ian didn't swing his leg forward. He went back to standing there impassively.

"*If you don't leave,*" Ian's voice was so calm it made a chill run up my spine, "*I will kill you right now. I will kick you until you are dead. And I won't make it quick. I will make sure that you feel the most exquisitely excruciating pain until the very last moments before you die. I will make sure you feel every single kick. I don't want to. But I will. You are done here.*"

His father held his arms up in defensive fear for a few moments, then he gave the smallest of nods. Ian started to walk away. Then he stopped himself.

"*If I ever see you again...*" His voice quivered for a moment, but he stopped and collected himself, "*...I better never see you again. I'm done fighting you. So, if I have to do it again—*"

"*I'm leaving!*" His father growled.

Ian looked at his father with that blank face for the longest of moments, nodded, then went to the porch steps and grabbed ahold of his mother. He laced one of his mother's arms over his shoulders and helped her into the house. Then the door closed. I watched for an hour, waiting for his father to get up. When he finally did, he cursed at the house, at Ian. But he got his keys out of the grass, climbed into his truck, and peeled out of the driveway, screaming the whole way. I watched his taillights disappear in the dark.

I was about to move away from the tree when Ian's house door opened again. His eyes went right to me. In the light coming from the house, I could see the tear tracks on his cheeks. And then he collapsed, falling to his ass right there in the doorway, his back against the doorjamb. I started to run to him, but he held up a hand. He looked over at me, tears in his eyes, and shook his head. I nodded. Then I walked around the tree and sat down where he could see me, my back against the trunk of it.

Ian sat in the doorway of his house until the sky was turning reddish pink, crying. I sat by the tree trunk and let him just not be alone. When dawn started to approach, he finally rose to his feet and wiped his nose with the back of his hand. I stood up from my spot by the tree. Ian chewed his lip, his eyes puffy and swollen from all of the crying. He looked over at me and mouthed the words "thank you." Then he went inside. And I went home.

When school started the next day, I was leaning back against my locker, waiting for Ian. I was going to stand by my locker until he walked into the school, even if he was late and the bell rang. I was going to see my friend walk into school, unbruised, liberated, and ready to start his last year of high school. When he walked into school, ten minutes before first bell, he was wearing the shirt that I had given him after I had ripped his and doctored his cut eyebrow. It was tight on him...but in the best of ways. He didn't walk down the middle of the hall, he walked down the side I was on. Other students still scurried out of his way, but he ignored it like always. When he passed me, he raised his hand and gave me the lightest tap against my cheek as he gave me a small smile. His feet never stopped moving.

As he walked away, I smiled widely, and Kyle, who had been leaning against his locker next to me, looked at me with wide, fearful eyes. I just shrugged and pushed away from my locker. *"That's like the Mafia's kiss of death, man!"* He rushed to walk beside me. *"He's probably going to kick your ass now. What did you do to piss him off??"* I rolled my eyes. *"Oh, fuck off, Kyle."* He sputtered as I walked away. I grabbed Kevin around his shoulders as he was stepping away from his locker. *"Walk me to class?"* I asked him as I led him down the hall. *"Shuh-shuh-sure, Muh-Mike."* He beamed at me.

"Do you want to be my friend?" I asked. *"Not just at lunch?"*

Kevin beamed. *"Yuh-yeah, man!"*

"I'm honored." I smiled. *"I need a real friend during the school year."*

It was a little cheesy and embarrassing, but Kevin didn't stop smiling all of senior year. We talked in classes, walked together between classes, did homework together, played video games at each other's houses, went to football games together and cheered with the other students, went and got pizza together, stayed at each other's houses. Besides Ian, Kevin became my best friend. Of course, Ian wasn't my best friend. He was more than that. Kevin could never replace or threaten my relationship with Ian. But...he made my life immeasurably better during my senior year.

Of course, I didn't hang out with Ian during senior year. I only saw him in the hallways and lunchroom at school. But he always made sure to at least lock eyes with me for a moment. To acknowledge me. It wasn't what I wanted—but I had made my own promise. I would give him this last year. I found out through other people that Ian took a job at the store shortly after school started. He did the stocking, sweeping, cleaning, sometimes running the cash register. His father had just up and left town for some reason, so Ian and his mom needed the extra money. Of course, I never had any idea why that happened when everyone sat around talking, inviting others to speculate. Sometimes I'd wander into the store. I always bought an iced tea, a lemonade, and dill pickle sunflower seeds when Ian was working the cash register. Then, for some reason, I'd stupidly forget them on the counter.

The first time I forgot my purchases, Ian hollered after me. When I turned, he indicated the drinks and sunflower seeds. I looked at the paid-for items on the counter blankly. Then I looked up at him and said: *"I don't really like those. But they're already paid for...so someone should enjoy them."* He chewed at his lip when I smiled, nodded, and left. I did this every time he was working the register.

I was letting him have his year, he let me have this.

"We hope to see you again." That's what Ian said every time after that first time. And every time, I'd turn at the door and say: *"Nothing could keep me away."*

Once, Kevin and I went to the store together. Kevin talked to Ian the entire time, but I kept my mouth shut and just stared at Ian. The way his jawbone looked each time he replied to Kevin. The way his dark hair was cut much shorter than during the summer. The way his button nose wiggled when he smiled at Kevin. His beautiful lips forming his words. Those icebergs floating in milky pools. I had to leave the store before Kevin and Ian were done talking.

Ian asked huh-how you were doing. Kevin frowned as we walked away from the store together afterward. *What did you say?* I had asked. *I suh-said you were the buh-best fuh-friend I'd ever had.* Kevin blushed. *I duh-didn't nuh-know you were fuh-friends.* I thought about this for several moments as we walked. *We aren't.* I responded. Which was true. "Friends" wasn't a big enough word for what we were. Kevin watched me out of the corner of his eye for a long time. Then he seemed to decide on something and dropped it.

Right before spring break of senior year, I opened my locker to find a folded-up piece of paper laying haphazardly on top of my stack of books. I immediately recognized the color and texture of the paper. My breath caught in my throat and my hands shook as I reached out to unfold it. It was a sketch of the "room" of wisteria—and it was breathtaking. He had sketched this from memory, and it was exactly as I remembered it. I could practically smell the wisteria as I looked at the sketch. On the back, Ian had written: *Late at night, when I'm in bed, and I feel all alone, I think of this. I got into Columbia University. X*

My heart filled. It ached. It broke. The end was coming.

Chapter 10

Ian

Mike's arms went around me, and his hands shot to my ass. Then he was lifting me in the water and I instinctively wrapped my legs around his waist tightly. My legs pulled him into me as my mouth worked to devour his. The Full Strawberry Moon shone down on us as my body moved desperately against his, rubbing against him as he held onto my ass, his fingers digging at my soft flesh through my swimsuit. I wanted to bite and suck at his neck, lick at his collarbone, feel the flesh of his chest and stomach against my lips—places lower. But I didn't want to take my lips from his mouth.

Jerkily, Mike walked towards shore, carrying me along as I fed at his mouth. Then We collapsed against the bank and he urged me upwards. I practically crawled back up the bank while trying to keep my mouth on his. Mike was moaning like an animal as he pushed against me and I crab-walked up the creek bank. When we reached the top of the embankment, his body pushed into mine until my shoulder blades were digging into the dirt and his pelvis was grinding into mine.

I wrapped my arms around him and flipped us over, my body coming to rest on top of his, my knees moving up to straddle him.

"*Oh, my God.*" Mike moaned into my mouth as I humped against him.

"*I want you.*" I breathed against his mouth as my hips continued to move. "*I've always wanted you. All of you.*"

Mike's arms were around me and I was suddenly rolled onto my stomach and Mike was sliding down my body. I felt his tongue against my calf, sliding up desperately, over the back of my thigh, my ass, my lower back. I moaned loudly, not giving a shit if anyone might be walking in the woods and would then come to investigate. His tongue slid up my spine, working its way up the valley of my back, then my neck. He roughly rolled me over until I was on my back, looking up into his face, more aroused than I had ever been in my life.

Mike pinned me down with his lower body, his hands holding my wrists as he looked down at me. I lifted my head, trying to get at his mouth. He'd start to lean down to meet my mouth, then pull back with an evil grin. I was sure that I looked like a snapping turtle, nipping at his mouth, but I didn't care. My body was aching for him and my mind was possessed by someone I hadn't allowed myself to be for four years.

"You've made your point," I growled. *"Put your fucking mouth on mine."*

We both knew that I could overpower Mike if I really wanted to—but I wanted to do this his way. I wanted to feel what he had been forced to hold back for four years. I wanted to give him that. And I wanted him to show me how he had imagined this going for that whole time.

"Say it again." He rolled his hips into mine.

"Say what?" I moaned as my mouth reached for him again.

He cocked an eyebrow at me.

"I love you, Mike." I breathed out.

Then his mouth was on mine and his hands moved away from my wrists so that I could wrap my arms around his wet back.

"I've always loved you, Mike," I said as my mouth moved to his neck.

We became a flurry of arms and legs and lips and teeth and every other body part, right there on the bank of our creek. The Full Strawberry Moon shone down on us, letting us see each other clearly as we crossed the four-year-long space between us. Our bodies became one as every part of our bodies worked together to finally express our feelings for each other. I lost all track of time as Mike's body became part of mine, and then mine became part of him, and our mouths touched every part of each other.

When the sky started turning violet, then red, getting closer to pink, we found ourselves wrapped tightly together, our legs and arms tucked tightly around each other, my head on Mike's chest. His eyes were closed, but his wide smile and soft breathing let me know that he wasn't asleep. He was in complete and utter rhapsody, his mind replaying the last few hours in his head as we lay there, dirty, wet, and not giving a damn about any of it.

"It'll be light soon," I whispered into his chest, my lips brushing against his skin as I smiled.

"I already see you just fine." Mike breathed into my hair.

"I wouldn't mind seeing more of you," I replied.

"You can see as much of me as you want as often as you want."

Though we were both smiling, our bodies satisfied—for the moment—the future still loomed. The light of summer only lasts so long. I moved my head up to kiss Mike gently on the lips. He wrapped his arms around me and held me to him as he returned the kiss. Then he allowed me to move down to kiss his neck, the front of his throat, his chest.

"I'll be back," I whispered to him.

"I'm not leaving," he said.

"Is that a promise?" I bit at my lower lip with a smile.

"I'd promise you the moon and then find a way to deliver, Ian." He opened his eyes to stare at me.

I nodded.

Mike laid back on the creek bed as I stood, still naked as the day I was born and shimmied down into the creek again. I stood there for a moment, letting my eyes drift up and down his naked body, taking him in as he seemed to glow beneath the wakening daylight. Happiness welled up inside of me, as though coming up through the Earth, through my legs, seeking out my chest. I waded out into the middle of the creek and looked up at the lightening sky, then laid back until I was floating. My legs went out straight and I held my arms out, floating perpendicular to my body. And I asked God for a talk. Not just a talk—but also a response. And for the first time since I'd come to talk to God at the creek—Mike's and my creek—God answered.

It was time to end this friendship.

Chapter 11

Mike
4 Years Later

I sat on the bank of the creek. High school students still had a week to go before school let out for summer. I was going to turn twenty-three soon. Time had flown by, but things remained the same there in my tiny little podunk Texas town. Though, for the most part, it hadn't been my town for four years. Austin had been my town. That's where the University of Texas is located, and that's where I went to college. So, that had been my home for the better part of those four years. I only got to come home during the summers. There was no reason to come home for Christmas or spring break. My life was in Austin.

Seeing my creek—mine and Ian's creek—made my eyes water and my chest puff up with emotion. This might be the very last time that I laid eyes on our creek. The creek was all that remained of our friendship. It was the one place I could go and remember the last time that we had been friends. The summers we had spent obsessed with each other. The night and morning we had spent wrapped up in each other. Sharing our bodies with each other, right here on this creek bed. Before Ian had waded out of the creek, dripping wet, completely naked, a look on his face that I had never seen before.

I don't want us to be friends anymore, Mike.

That's what he had said when he came to stand at my feet and looked down at my naked body. My eyes had shot open to look up at him. The sun had risen enough that it was behind his head, casting him in a halo, making his face dark and unreadable. It was the worst moment of my life. I'd had bad moments in my life before that morning—but those words broke my heart in a way that nothing else ever had. I knew it had been coming—but I hadn't prepared myself for it—wanting to believe that things would turn out okay. Those words, coming from the best friend I'd ever had until that moment, shattered me to the core.

Now I sat there on that creek bank, where I had first asked Ian to be my friend. He had said yes. The creek bank where he saw me for the first time, memorized my face and body, and sketched me from memory. The creek bank where he taught me so many things about life. The creek bank where we crawled out, soaking wet, our mouths trying to devour each other. Where we made love under the Full Strawberry Moon. The creek bank where I could still feel everything I had loved about my friendship with Ian.

Ian Chambers.
Ian Chambers.
Ian Chambers.
That was his whole name.
Ian Chambers.
Righter of wrongs. Protector of the weak.
Brave.
Selfless.
Tough.
Kissable lips.

The reason why God made the days of summer so long. Provided so much light. So that we could see each other clearly. I looked down, tears falling from my eyes as I thought of Ian. Thought about how I may never see this creek again. How I could never hold Ian's hands, look up and watch the bats hunt for their dinner. Hold hands and take in the full moon. Hold his hands and tell him that I loved him. That would never happen in this creek again.

And I had to be okay with that.

There was nothing that could be done.

I had made my promises, too.

And, like Ian, I was a man of my word.

"I got the car packed."

I smiled at the voice, my eyes closing languidly.

"Are you sleeping?"

Laughter.

The most wonderful laughter in the world.

"No," I responded, my eyes fluttering open as I turned my head. "I was just trying to memorize everything about our creek."

Ian looked down at me. He had been ready to go. He'd been waiting for four years, after all.

"We can stay a little longer." He sat down beside me, pulling his knees up to his chest, wrapping his arms around them. "Law school isn't going anywhere."

"Columbia's been waiting for four years." I tilted my body to lay my head against his shoulder. "If you blow them off for law school, too, they'll never readmit you."

"We'll get Principal Morton to pull more strings." Ian laughed.

"You were lucky with U of T, babe." I laughed with him. "I don't think he has any 'strings' at Columbia."

He turned his head to give me a soft kiss and a smile.

"I'll miss our creek, too," he said softly.

I nodded, turning my head back to look at the creek again. The crystal-clear water bathed in the early morning light. Just like it had been on the morning Ian walked out of the creek naked and told me he didn't want to be my friend anymore. That that wasn't good enough. He wanted to be my everything. And he wanted me to be the same for him. He wanted to give himself over to me completely. And nothing else mattered as much as that. Not even Columbia.

My shattered heart came back together, larger and healthier than it had been before. Sometimes...*sometimes*...being broken and put back together makes a person stronger and happier than ever. It was true for my heart—and it had been true for Ian. Four years of being with him in Austin, going to classes at the University of Texas with him, where I never had a chance of keeping up with him academically, going to bed with him each night—when we slept—and waking up, wrapped in his arms, every morning. All of it had been more than my heart could hold. But I refused to let go of any of it. Every bit of Ian, everything that we'd done together, that we would do together, would stay there until my heart was no longer. I promised myself that.

Ian had taught me to keep promises.

"Did you stop at the store?" I asked, my lips against his shoulder.

"Not yet," he said. "I thought you might want to come along."

"Is he still there?" I chuckled.

"Well, not for long," Ian replied. "He graduated, too. So, he'll be getting a better job soon, I'm sure."

I looked at the creek.

"You couldn't just enroll at U of T law school?" I teased.

"You gave me four years of high school." He looked at me with a cocked eyebrow. "I gave you four of college. Now, I get three for law school."

"Do I get three after that?" I wiggled my eyebrows.

"Only if you use them well." He laughed.

"Oh, I can think of a few ways to use them."

"Come on, you horny bastard." Ian stood, holding his hand out to me. "But, I guess, if you give me three years for law school, I can give you three years of uninterrupted, unbridled, passionate sex."

I rolled my eyes. "Like you aren't dying to."

Ian pulled me in roughly and shoved his mouth over mine. And, for the last time, we kissed each other on the bank of our creek. When we parted, Ian laced his fingers through mine and pulled me toward the woods. We walked through the woods together, stopping every few yards to kiss each other. When we made our way out of the woods, we jumped into my car, buckled our seatbelts, then looked at each other and took a deep breath.

"Store?"

"Store." I nodded.

Ian drove us to the store, and we got back out of the car. Hand in hand, in that piece of shit Texas town, we walked into the store. Two gay men, who had loved each other for eight years, no longer caring what the jerks in the town thought of...*anything*.

"Luh-look at you assholes." I smiled at the voice.

Kevin was standing behind the register, his arms folded over his chest.

"Who are you calling an asshole, douchebag?" I smiled back at him.

Kevin just smiled at us, the two of us holding hands not a surprise to him at all. He had seen us numerous times over the last four years. Kevin knew that Ian and I had never been friends. We'd always been so much more.

"Is it tuh-time already?" Kevin's smile turned sad.

"It's time, man." I nodded slowly.

"I'll muh-miss you guh-guys." He came from around the register.

He pulled me into a hug, then Ian. Unlike the other assholes in town, he didn't give a shit that we were together. We were his friends. The best friends that he had ever had. And in turn, he had been one of the best friends to us. Ian grabbed Kevin's face in his hands and looked him in the eyes.

"I'm going to miss you, man." Ian's eyes were watery.

"It's nuh-not too hard to buh-buy a plane ticket to New York." Kevin smiled. "Or to tuh-Texas."

"You'll always have a place on our couch, Kevin," I said for the two of us.

"Same huh-here." He hugged both of us again.

I left Ian to talk to Kevin as I grabbed the things that we needed. Luckily, the store was empty, so Kevin and Ian's conversation wasn't interrupted until I came back to the register, my cart loaded up. Kevin checked us out as he and Ian continued talking. Finally, we were checked out and all of our groceries bagged up. And it was time to go. Kevin did his best to smile—but it wasn't his best effort. When Ian and I headed for the door, Ian looked just as torn. But Columbia was waiting after all.

"Will you tell your brother I said 'hi?'" Ian asked with an evil grin.

"Just to puh-piss him off, muh-man." Kevin grinned back.

"We'll see you soon. Right?" Ian's eyes were leaking.

"You cuh-couldn't keep me away." Kevin smiled widely.

So, we left. We packed up the car with the bags of groceries, got back into our seats, buckled our belts, and Ian's head turned to me. He grabbed my hand nervously and squeezed it.

"Do you...do you think it'll be okay?" He looked down, unsure of himself for once. "I'm nervous."

"I'll be there." I squeezed his hand back. "And whatever happens, happens."

He watched me for a moment, then nodded once. Ian started the car, and we began the drive across town. We drove down backroad after backroad, over bumpy, pothole-riddled roads, until finally, we pulled up in front of the dinky little shack in the woods. Ian let out a shaky breath, so I reached over and gave his hand another squeeze.

"It'll be okay," I said.

"Okay."

We got out, each of us taking three bags apiece, and headed toward the porch. When we walked up the steps, the door opened before we could get up onto the porch. Carson looked the same...but with a beard. His eyes looked confused at first, then there was that moment of recognition. Ian froze. I looked at the love of my life, then at Carson.

"What are you doing here?" Carson asked, his eyes suddenly on his feet.

Ian looked down at his feet, too.

I waited, but they both just looked at their feet and stayed silent.

"We're going to New York," I said finally. "Columbia. Ian's going to law school."

I knew that Ian had been coming to bring groceries to Carson's house during school breaks. He couldn't do it as often as he had wanted, but he still brought them when he could. He wouldn't be able to anymore.

"You always were so damn smart, man," Carson said, but his eyes stayed down. "As smart as you were tough."

"Not as tough as you, man," Ian replied, his eyes staying down as well. "You're a tough son of a bitch."

Carson looked up, his eyes red.

"Thank you," Carson said.

They were both silent again.

"We wanted to bring you these," I said, jiggling the bags lightly in my arms. "Thought you might not have a lot of time to get to the store."

Carson looked over at me, as though he had forgotten I was there, then looked down again.

"Kevin's still around," I said evenly. "He said that he'd be happy to go to the store for you if you wanted some help."

Carson looked up, his eyes leaking now, too.

"He's a really good cook." I continued. "And he's not afraid of some yard work...if you ever needed help getting stuff done."

"*He'd do that?*" Carson whispered down at the porch.

Ian was still holding the bags, looking down.

"All you have to do is call him." I nodded. "He's also exceptionally good at being a friend. Best one I ever had, besides Ian."

When Kevin had found out about Carson from me, during our freshman year at U of T, he didn't say "good" or "serves him right" or anything you'd expect. He'd only said: "is there anything I can do to help?" I had told him that if anything came up, I'd let him know. When I told him that Carson might need someone for support now that Ian wouldn't be dropping things off periodically, he said he'd be happy to help him. Kevin was a good guy. And underneath everything, so was Carson. They could probably be really good friends.

"I'd like that." Carson looked up, clearing his throat.

"I'll give you his number." I smiled. "So...can we carry these in for you?"

Carson seemed to choke a little, then gave a nod. And the three of us carried the groceries into the house. Ian was silent as he helped unpack the groceries, but I did my best to keep a conversation going as Carson helped me figure out where each item went. When we were done putting up the groceries, Carson said his father was napping, so he had time if we wanted something to drink. We all had coffee out on the porch, where Ian stayed silent, barely looking up as I did my best to have a conversation with Carson.

Then it became apparent that it was time for us to leave and get on the road. I reminded Carson that Kevin was in the area still if he ever needed help or an ear. I gave him Kevin's number and gave him ours too, just in case he thought we could help him in any way. I gave him a quick handshake and headed toward the car after saying my "goodbyes." Carson held a hand out to Ian. Ian looked at him for a minute, then pulled Carson into a hug. It took a moment since Carson was so shocked, but he returned the hug. They still didn't say anything, but when they ended the hug, they looked at each other for a long time, still holding onto each other. Carson gave Ian a nod and a small smile and Ian returned the gesture.

Ian and I got in the car and waved back to Carson before turning the car around and driving away from the shack in the woods. When we got on the highway, the early afternoon sun was beating down on us as we drove away from a place we never intended to return to—at least, not permanently. But, where there are friends, there's always a place to visit.

"I love you." Ian reached over to take my hand while his other hand steered the car. "I really love you, Mike."

"How long have you loved me?" I smirked at him.

"Since that time you saw the squirrel and worried that it was dead." He smiled widely. "Since I saw your heart."

"When didn't you love me?" I asked.

"When I didn't know you existed." He replied. "Once I knew you existed, there wasn't a time that I didn't love you."

I smiled at him.

"I've loved you since I first saw the light of the sun, felt its warmth," I replied. "Because I knew that it was telling me that you were coming."

Ian pulled my hand up to his mouth and kissed the back of it. And we drove away from that Podunk town in Texas, on our way to a better life. A life where there would never be long months of cold and dark and loneliness, with only the light of summer to make everything better. Every day would be light and warm. Every day would be ours.

A Surplus of Light

The following is a short story that first appeared in 'Four Short Stories from the Books of Chase Connor' – which is no longer in print. It tells the story of Ian and Mike's first meeting at the tree by the creek—but from Ian's perspective. Hopefully, you will enjoy it.

Additionally, a follow-up story to A SURPLUS OF LIGHT, titled A SPECIES OF SPECIAL CONCERN, can be found on Chase Connor Books.

You can find it here:

https://chaseconnor.com/2021/05/18/a-species-of-special-concern/

Tremendous Love & Thanks,
Chase

Squirrels generally do not make great models. They move a lot. They're nervous little balls of anxiety, always hyper-aware and paranoid. But, as I was sitting against the tree by the creek, my sketchpad laid against my knees, wondering what I should sketch, a squirrel sauntered up lazily and threw himself down on the large, flat rock at the creek's edge. He looked like he had fallen in the creek and had struggled to extricate himself. He was tuckered out. He just wanted to sun himself. His head had lolled to the side when he first laid down and he eyed me for a moment. After a few moments, he decided that I was not going to bother him, so he went to sleep. I started to sketch.

Trees were usually my favorite subject because they're not known for moving around much, are they? Other plants, flowers, landscapes, they were pretty good for sketching for the same reason. Sometimes, I'd get lucky and one of the kids at the creek would sit still long enough that I could sketch them quickly. But those sketches were never that great because the kids never stayed still long enough for a *real* sketch to be done. Except for the kid with the sandy blonde hair and mossy green eyes and the beginnings of freckles along his nose. Michael Steedman.

That was his name.

I had asked Kevin when I ran into him at the creek once.

Kevin knew everyone and everyone knew Kevin, though he didn't really have many friends. He wanted to be my friend, but...but that just wasn't a great idea. If Kevin was going to make one friend, it was best if it wasn't me. Too much baggage there. No reason to put another target on Kevin's back. He got heckled for his stutter and being scrawny enough. He didn't need his friendship with a *bad kid* to be another reason that he got bullied. Of course, no one bullied Kevin much anymore. And I doubted that his most persistent bully, Carson, was going to bother him much anymore, either. At least not as frequently. Carson had probably learned his lesson when I had hit him.

I felt my eyes start to water at the memory.

I clenched my hand, flexing my fingers as I looked down at the bruises that littered my knuckles.

I hated my hands.

I hated violence.

I hated that my hands could be used for both the kindest and cruelest of touches.

I hated that people were capable of such cruelty.

I hated being...alone.

Clearing my throat, I moved my shaking hand back to the sketchpad, took a deep breath, steadied my hand, and continued sketching the squirrel. I forced myself to smile over at the squirrel, thankful for such an unexpected and wonderful subject. Living things usually don't give me the opportunity to sketch them. Sure, it was just a squirrel...no, not *just a squirrel*...it was a living creature that had honored me with its fearless presence. This squirrel had sensed that I was harmless. It knew that I would do nothing to harm it as long as it didn't harm me. For that, I was incredibly grateful. I felt exalted. That made me blush and feel embarrassed at my unearned pride.

I didn't feel so alone with the squirrel sleeping on the warm rock, sunning itself dry. Something had chosen to spend time with me, even if it was at a short distance. He didn't mind me, and I didn't mind him. We were able to sit there in silence together, both of us doing what was second nature to us. And we allowed each other to do that without interference or judgment.

When Michael Steedman approached, I heard and sensed him rather than saw him. I knew, after a week of being stalked by him, that Michael would eventually approach me. For a solid week, every time I looked up, there he was, watching me, examining me, trying to figure me out. At the creek. In the store. Walking along the streets. Sitting by my favorite tree along the wooded path where I loved to sketch and watch animals. He always seemed to find me...and his eyes did a number on me each time. I didn't mind so much. I did mind that he never said anything. Then again, he had witnessed me hitting Carson, so he was probably keeping a safe distance.

I couldn't blame him.

For the first few days, anyway.

After a week, it was making me sad to see him watching me yet saying nothing. Of course, I didn't really want him to say anything. Or did I? He was a popular kid at school. He didn't need me bringing down his social stock. Of course, a kid like Michael Steedman probably wouldn't get bullied much, if at all, if he was friends with me. He was one of those kids who could do whatever he wanted, and people still thought the sun shined out of his ass. I usually hated people like that. But not Michael Steedman. He always said "hello" to Kevin in the hallways and smiled at him, even though they weren't friends. He never picked on other kids or was cruel. He never jumped out of my way like other kids did. Of course, he didn't seem too aware that I existed, either. Not until he saw me sketching by the creek. He was blissfully unaware of most things that went on around him, consumed by his own life.

And his life probably wasn't all that fantastic.

Just average.

When Michael Steedman approached me at the edge of the creek, as I sat there sketching the squirrel, he stopped before he got too close. I continued to sketch for a moment, waiting for him to say something. To give him the option of whether or not he wanted to pursue...whatever it was he was pursuing. After a few moments, it became apparent that even today, with no other kids around, he was doubting whether or not he should talk to me. Whether or not he should be afraid of me. So...I went against my nature. I gave a kid a break.

I looked up at him but didn't stop sketching.

He looked...shocked?

"You still stalking me?" I asked before turning my attention back to my squirrel sketch. *"I thought you'd have given up by now."*

I somehow kept myself from smiling as he walked in a wide arc around me, afraid to get too close. Afraid to enter my atmosphere, as though the gravity of who I was would pull him in and never let him leave.

"What are you always drawing?" He asked.

Then he sat down a few feet away in front of me, his back to the rock and the squirrel, not noticing it at all. Blissfully unaware. The squirrel hadn't spooked at Michael Steedman's approach. That was...*interesting.*

"Usually trees," I answered, looking back up at him. His eyes were so green. Mossy. Kind. *"Sometimes other kids. Birds. That squirrel there."*

I flicked my head in the direction of the squirrel, my bangs landing in my eyes. As Michael Steedman turned his head slowly to look at the squirrel, I reached up and pushed my dark hair out of my eyes again. Suddenly, Michael Steedman's eyes grew wide, and he looked devastated.

"*Is he dead?*"

I don't know how to explain what happened to me then. But my heart felt like it swelled until it was pushing against my ribcage. My chest felt full. It was hard to breathe for a moment. Did he really care if this squirrel was dead? God, I hoped that he did. I took pity on Michael Steedman and swallowed hard, then squealed loudly, even though I knew I'd lose my sketch subject. The squirrel popped up on his hindquarters, its head whipping back and forth frantically. Its eyes went to both of the boys sitting by it, then it dashed off quickly in a blur of fur.

"*He was just sunning himself,*" I said.

Michael Steedman gave a relieved chuckle.

There went my heart again.

"*What have you got there?*" I asked, nodding at the bag he had set down beside himself.

"*I, uh, brought us some sodas and chips.*" He was blushing. "*If you want some anyway.*"

Michael Steedman had ventured out to the creek to find me. He assumed that he would bring snacks and he would talk to me and we'd become best friends. He would open up to this strange, violent, bad kid who sketched things, and we would suddenly be tied at the hip. He was right.

"*I don't eat,*" I said.

He was frowning at me.

"*Or drink,*" I added. "*I consume the blood of virgins and smoke the reefer and I joined a gang right before school last year. Sometimes you can see me swimming at the creek at night, worshipping Satan.*"

153

Okay. Maybe that made me an asshole. But I knew that Michael Steedman had heard the rumors about me. I knew that other kids had told him that I was a *bad kid* who did horrible things. It didn't matter that none of it was true. I wanted to test his mettle.

"Is any of that true?" He asked after staring at me for several breathless moments.

I stared back at him, wondering if this kid, Michael Steedman, believed these things when he had heard them from others. Or had he thought it was all bullshit until he heard me say them? Would he be my friend either way? Internally, I knew it didn't matter if he'd be my friend if they were true—because they weren't. But I would rather be alone than have a friend who would judge me. However, I realized that Michael Steedman had come to the creek with sodas and chips, determined to be my friend no matter what. So...I was going to be nice.

"I like swimming at night." I nodded. *"But I don't believe in Satan. And it's kind of hard to find a virgin nowadays."*

"Why does everyone say those things about you?" He laughed nervously.

It was adorable. Michael Steedman was nervous and shy. I didn't really have that effect on a lot of people. Mostly they were scared of me—either because they'd heard stories or just assumed things about me. Michael Steedman, though, he seemed self-conscious.

"Carson, the guy you saw me with the other day?"

He nodded, not bothering to lie and say that he hadn't been spying on me a week prior. I liked that he didn't try to deny it.

"That's not the first time I've had to punch him. After the first time, he started making up stories about me. He didn't realize that it made no difference to me."

"I guess he never learns." Michael Steedman smiled and looked down.

Michael Steedman.

Michael Steedman.

Michael Steedman.

I kept saying his name in my head. Michael Steedman was an All-American boy. Blond, built, gorgeous. Easy smile. Affable. Kind. An "aw-shucks" type of guy. The type of guy you'd pay a compliment to and he'd reach up and rub the back of his neck while looking down at his feet while he blushed and smiled. He was absolutely adorable, and my stomach felt like butterflies. I knew exactly what that meant. And it scared the shit out of me.

"I don't like hurting people. No matter what you might have heard." I was mentally pleading with him.

Don't. Judge. Me.

Michael Steedman's eyes flicked down to my hands. They were covered in bruises, but I did nothing to hide that fact.

"I believe you." It was an exhalation.

I found myself staring at this All-American Boy, body of a god, looks that most guys would kill for...and I believed that he believed me. After several moments, I realized that staring much longer would probably scare him away, and I didn't want that. I stretched my legs out and let my sketchpad lay upon them as I smiled at Michael Steedman.

"So, what kinds of chips and soda did you bring?"

"I, uh, didn't know what you'd like, so I just got Cokes and a couple of bags of Cheetos." He replied nervously, removing the items from the bag.

I hated Cokes and Cheetos. But I was touched by the thought.

"*Perfect.*" It was a harmless lie. "*But I don't have any money.*"

"*It's cool.*" He feigned insouciance. "*I had some allowance saved up.*"

I doubted he had to save up allowance. His parents probably gave him money anytime he wanted or needed it. I didn't hold that against him. That was nice. But I thought about that for a moment. One should never go into a relationship without being on an even keel. I didn't want to owe Michael Steedman anything, even if he probably wouldn't hold that over my head. I flipped through my sketchpad, found the sketch I was looking for, ripped it out, and held it out to him.

"*We're even.*"

Michael Steedman took the sketch from me gently, his eyes staying on mine as he pulled the sketch close to himself. His mossy green eyes stayed on mine, his affable and gentle and kind nature shining through until the sketch was right under his face. He looked down at the sketch and his eyes immediately widened and lit up, the smallest, self-conscious smile appearing on his lips.

"*Wow,*" he said simply as he looked down at the sketch I had done of him the first time I had laid eyes on him, sitting across the creek from me a week prior.

"*It's not my best,*" I admitted as I moved to grab the Coke and Cheetos that he had bought for me. "*But it's not my worst.*"

"*It's...amazing.*" Michael Steedman looked up at me, his smile no longer self-conscious.

"*Thank you.*" I twisted the cap off of my Coke. "*I like your hair. You should let it grow out even more.*"

Michael Steedman's hair begged to have fingers run through it. It was like the sun as it just started to peek over the horizon at dawn. Warm and golden and beautiful.

"*So...what's your name?*" He asked.

I couldn't help myself. My eyebrow rose as I sized him up. Did he think that I'd believe that he hadn't heard about me?

"*Okay.*" He was blushing, aware that that had been a poor attempt at subterfuge.

"*And you're Michael Steedman.*"

Saying the name out loud made my stomach flip-flop.

"*Mike.*" He interjected, still blushing. "*I go by 'Mike' to everyone but my mom.*"

"*What does your mom call you, Mike?*" I smiled, curious to know what nickname he'd been saddled with as I brought my soda to my lips.

"*Sugar Man, mostly.*" He blushed so deeply that I wanted to pull him into me and laugh and hug him and make him feel less self-conscious.

Mostly, I wanted to thank him for being so unabashedly honest.

Instead, I just grinned.

"*You look like a 'baby boy' or 'junior' to me, personally,*" I said, honestly having thought that one of those would have been the nickname. "*Sugar Man doesn't really fit you.*"

That was the truth. He didn't look like a "Sugar Man." He was too...*Michael Steedman* for such a "squee" name.

He laughed gently, the blush slowly fading from his face.

"*But there are worse things than 'Sugar Man,' I guess.*" I shrugged.

"*Do you want to be my friend?*" Mike spat suddenly, then blushed again, his eyes dropping to look at his lap.

I held my breath, the weight of this moment in my chest. The absolute joy at having Mike Steedman find me by the creek, doing something so thoughtful as bringing me food and drink. Talking to me like I was a normal person. Not being scared of me. Not treating me like a bad kid. Wanting to be my friend.

"*All right.*" I nodded.

"*Good.*" He smiled and reached for his Cheetos excitedly.

I breathed out, trying to not show how excited I was that Mike had sought me out and asked to be my friend. And I was so grateful. I would drink Coke and eat Cheetos and sit there and talk to Mike about anything he wanted to talk about. I wasn't alone anymore. Silently, I thanked God for two things as Mike began talking ninety-to-nothing. The squirrel. And Michael Steedman.

The End.

About the Author

Chase Connor his days writing about the people who live (loudly and rent-free) in his head when he's not busy being enthusiastic about naps and Pad Thai. Chase started his writing career as a confused gay teen looking for an escape from reality. Ten years later, one of the books he wrote during those years, *Just A Dumb Surfer Dude: A Gay Coming-of-Age Tale*, was published independently. Now with The Lion Fish Press (and 20 books later), Chase has numerous projects in various stages of completion lined up for publishing. Chase is a multi-genre author, but always with a healthy dollop of gay.

Chase can be reached at
chaseconnor@chaseconnor.com
Or on Twitter **@ChaseConnor7**
He can also be found on Chase Connor Books
https://chaseconnor.com
or on Goodreads
https://www.goodreads.com/author/show/18055910.Chase_Connor

He does his very best to respond to all DMs, emails, and Twitter comments from his reader friends and loves the interaction with them. Chase has several novellas/novels for sale on Amazon (and other sites) in ebook and paperback format.

Chase Connor's catalog can be read for free with Kindle Unlimited

Made in the USA
Coppell, TX
27 September 2022

83692774R00100